CHUCKANUT DREAMS

MARTIN BROWN

ISBN: 978-1-5356-1185-5

Dedicated to

Mom, Dad, Brendan, Sara, Margaret,
Nora, Erin, Joe, Keara, Jet, Ryan
And, as always and forever,
Patti

Acknowledgements

The Marianist Community, a community of men who have dedicated themselves to a life of purpose and instilling strength in others.Dr. Ralph Vernacchia, Ph.D., renowned international sports psychologist, former coach of Western Washington University, and consultant to the 2000 U.S. Olympic Team.

Mr. Gerald O'Brien, a youth coach whom every youth should have.

The 1972 Team Canada Hockey team, a team who realized a dream and galvanized the better angels of the people of their country.

Bud Willis, head coach of London (Ontario, Canada) Legion Middle Distance, friend, and lifelong inspiration.

Hayley Wickenheiser, a hero who inspired women to have the same passion for excellence in hockey and sport that men had been afforded.

Diane O'Neill, A masterful educator who inspired the discipline of writing for so many.

"Thoughts lead on to purposes; purposes go forth in action; actions form habits; habits decide character; and character fixes our destiny."

— TYRON EDWARDS

Contents

Raised with Purpose 1

Transformation 9

Bennett 29

Acquired Notions 33

Brave New World 49

Happy Times 59

Rocking More Than the Obvious 75

Searching 79

Bloom off the Rose 83

Words Worth Their Weight 91

Truth Delayed 95

Embarrassment 97

Diversion 107

Whirlwind 111

Loving the Dream Chaser 115

Thunderstorms 121

Suffering 125

Aftermath 133

Deafening Sounds 139

Movement 145

Clueless 149

Foreclosure 153

Shattered Glass 159

Explosion 163

The Inevitable 167

Deceit 171

Double Standard 179

Driveway Depression 183

Nadir 189

Twists 193

Pragmatics 223

Epilogue 231

CHUCKANUT DREAMS

Raised with Purpose

"HENDERSON SCORES FOR CANADA." IT is said that anybody who had a pulse in Canada on that September day in 1972 knew the magnitude of that line delivered by iconic sports broadcaster Foster Hewitt. In the inaugural eight-game series between Russia and Canada, the Canadians battled back from a deficit to tie the series 3–3–1. In the eighth and final game, the hockey world witnessed a seesaw battle of two nations whose different political and cultural societies defined the world. Democracy and Communism. With the game being played in Moscow, the odds against the Canadians were overwhelming. Paul Henderson's shot with thirty seconds left won the game. Schools were shut down, work absentees were everywhere, as our whole nation watched it on CTV, witnessing and sharing in an inexplicable joy.

Worshiping other trivialities, my family was one of those rare Canadian families who did not know, understand, or care about the passion, patriotism, and pride that won that game for Team Canada. In Montreal they say "Hockey is life." I never knew or cared what that meant. It was only later on when I met a man whose very existence was a personification of all those things that I understood. In my little girl's world, I was yearning for a father. Early on we thought we found that man; he was a

1

hockey player, but hockey and Canada are only a part of this story. This is a human story.

While others in the North Vancouver, British Columbia, suburb of Delbrook were born with a silver spoon in their mouth, Jack McKenna came home to a crib on the snow-laden third day of that January adorned with his first wooden hockey stick, a gift from his uncle, "Uncle Mac" MacGregor Whately, a Canadian hockey legend. Whately, a pilot in the Royal Canadian Air Force, was a "behind-the-scenes driving force," for the assemblage of that force's team that won the 1948 Olympic gold medal in hockey. Although deadlocked with Czechoslovakia in a round-robin record of seven wins and one tie, the Canadians prevailed with their "goals for" and "goals against" averages.

McKenna's neighbor Jan Drobny, who had fled from Prague in 1968, always felt that political intrigue, not sport, "took the gold medal out from under the Czechs."

"Mr. Drobny, you know not of our special Canadian resiliency and strength of purpose."

"So you think it's something spezial?"

"Born out of our hard winters and pioneer spirit," Mac would tell his good friend, who'd craftily made his own escape from the communist country by bicycling over the Germany border as a teenager.

Whately, before serving his country in wartime, made himself wealthy by selling encyclopedias door-to-door. "There were only two Canadians who had the moxie and drive to make money doing that...Jack Kent Cooke and myself." Whately would often share "that fact" with any listener, modestly placing himself in a category with the wealthiest man in North America. He later made millions as proprietor of the original Canadian hockey equipment company, Hoquet. Hockey and Mother Canada ran blood-red in the veins of the Whatelys.

Jack's dad, a tavern owner in South Vancouver, succumbed to lung cancer when Jack was an infant. Every picture of him in the family home that lay in the shadow of the North Shore Mountains foreshadowed his short-lived years, as "Cleary" McKenna was never without a cigarette in his mouth.

Cleary's family had moved from County Wexford when he was three. To "Grandpa McKenna," who cherished the "intrigue of God's oceans," immigrating to Vancouver, a city surrounded by saltwater, was as good as being close to the Irish Sea. It was imbedded in the McKenna men that a few hours on a Sunday staring out to the English Bay was all the recreation a man needed, along with some "inspiring words from the greats of Eire."

"Other than reading the great Irish authors, Kavanagh, Behan, Joyce, and Shaw…a man should be indulged solely in his work and support of his family"—so barked the indomitable Grandpa McK. If a man ever "worked himself to death, that would be your father," according to Jack's mother, Marguerite Whately McKenna. When Cleary passed, Marguerite sold the tavern, financially supporting the family as a registered nurse at nearby Lions Gate Hospital, and emotionally supporting Jack and his brother through her unabated encouragement of their hockey years. Jack inherited his love for books from his mother, as she had an intense devotion to their education, and particularly to their reading and appreciation of literature.

The McKenna and Whately marriage was a unique mixing of families with patriotic fervor. The Whatelys had the innate sense of drive and labor, but there was an acceptable form of recreation—very acceptable. The Whatelys added the passion for hockey. Hockey, Family, and Canada were the altars they worshipped upon. Marguerite convinced Cleary to name Jack's older brother "Preston." It came from the name of the Preston Rivulettes, a renowned all-women's hockey team in the thirties. She didn't want that name that stood for grace, strength, and independence to be forgotten, at least in her family. In their early childhood, both boys' true home was the ice rink. The Whatelys were from a long line of rigid Scottish Presbyterians, but that religiosity was not as rigidly devoted for them as what went on within the parameters of a hockey rink.

Uncle Mac, opinionated, irascible, and self-admittedly "a tad stubborn," had the respect of Jack and his brother, as he naturally fell into the role of surrogate father to them. Before the boys were teenagers, they knew well the great noble history of their mother country, Canada. They were also treated to special morsels of what some of the neighborhood boys would call "Uncle Mac's patriotic paranoia."

Gathering the boys on the back porch and spitting out words of anger, Mac grizzled, "You young ones should know how Hollywood slighted the heroes of Canada in their greatest movie ever, *The Great Escape.*" With the boys' eyes ablaze with fire, Mac would go on, "The World War II escape blockbuster failed to mention the one hundred and fifty Canadians who helped dig the escape tunnels, including the legendary 'good friend' Royal Canadian Air Force pilot, Wally Floody, who orchestrated the whole plan."

Whately would get especially emotional when he spoke of how nearly two thirds of a force of five thousand brave Canadian soldiers were "sacrificed at Dieppe, France, so the Allied Forces could two years later succeed at the Normandy Invasion." While Mac tried, like most Canadians, not to show enmity toward his neighbors south of the border, he questioned the appreciation America showed their valiant neighbor to the north. Often in the eighties Mac would explode to anyone listening about the "lack of respect Canada received when their diplomat got a few American hostages safely out of Iran during the Iranian hostage crisis."

"Would those cowboys do the same for us if the situation were reversed?" Mac often queried.

Mac's affinity for both the game of hockey and the spirit imbued in it were legendary. "Don't think you boys are going to grow up without piano lessons," Mac famously once told his grandsons. Using the wall of Mac's Steinway piano before either of them reached nine as a makeshift goal, Jack and Preston had permission for what Mac referred to as his "piano lessons." By the time Jack was nine, it was clear he could outshoot and out-defend his older sibling in even neighborhood play. By the time Preston was twelve, he was no longer even interested in playing hockey with friends, and certainly not in the major junior leagues.

When he was young, Jack could never understand why his older brother he looked up to so much bowed out of the game so early. Jack's favorite picture from his youth was one his mother took at Grouse Mountain when Jack was five. In it Preston was all dressed in his hockey gear, and he was holding Jack tightly, tying his skates for him. Jack remembers the mountain, the mound of snow alongside the ice pond, and, most importantly, the memory of the momentary closeness he shared with his brother. That closeness was as fleeting as the frost that fell in a late Vancouver winter.

It was not so long after that picture was taken that anyone on ice with Jack could feel the wisp of the puck whizz by their skates, a puck sliced by this rising young phenom in the game. Ripping through the British Columbia Rep Leagues, Jack was growing up in the fabled Canadian Juniors. Jack billeted all over the Western provinces, a routine for all serious Canadian juniors. Writing to his mother from one of his first billets in Manitoba, Jack proclaimed, "It's 24/7 hockey and certainly nobody wants to discuss books, and certainly not Irish literature."

Jack continued to play flawlessly through the Junior A level, being considered "one of the country's top-ten major juniors to watch in 1978," according to *Slice Magazine*. Jack's puck-handling and speed on the ice earned him the nickname "The FOJ"…understood to be "The F— Offensive Juggernaut."

Often daydreaming of playing for one of the American universities with "ivy walls and huge American football stadiums," Jack was convinced that it would be better for his hockey future to stay in the Major Juniors. This would mean foregoing any kind of scholarship or chance to play south of the border. Enrolling as an English major at Simon Fraser University, Jack "went through the motions" as a student. He was now playing for the Coquitlam Rockets of the Western Hockey League. In 1978, the team was experiencing scheduling and financial difficulties and suspended play for the season.

While Uncle Mac and extended family worried about whether Jack would lose his conditioning edge, Jack breathed a sigh of relief. To Jack, this was an "omen" to do what he'd always felt he needed to do…spread his wings away from the umbilical cord he'd grown up with in Vancouver. While he loved playing for Coquitlam player/coach "Big Jim" McCutcheon, he felt "burnt out." McCutcheon, whose actual stint in the NHL was two lengthy games for the St. Louis Blues, knew well the fickle world of competitive hockey. McCutcheon had played in eight leagues during his dynamic hockey career, but seemed to be the personification of the idea that there was something greater than icing your way through cities, provinces, and life. McCutcheon decided to end his hockey career at the close of the 1977–1978 season. The team suspended play for the 1978–1979 season.

"It all seems like too much of a seesaw life," McCutcheon once intimated to Jack. "Maybe there's more than hockey out there. Maybe there's loyalty, teamwork, and passion that can be well put into something else, somewhere else." Those words stuck with Jack like a limb in his back.

Transformation

THE TERMINATION OF THE TEAM reinforced that reality to Jack. "This is an overdue omen that my hockey life is over!" His mother, lamenting the loss that seemed like a death in the family, was the first to express outrage at his decision.

Jack respectfully replied, "Mom, do you wish me to end up like Terry? Let's not forget how much pain and talent he gave to the game, and then they reduced him to a sketch of a freak on a *Life Magazine* cover. Worse than that, when he was beaten down playing for the Bruins, the brass and the press out there called him a quitter...you told me that, Mom."

Marguerite's distant cousin, Terry Sawchuk, was one of the greatest goalies ever to play the game. He ended up dying at forty, a four-time Stanley Cup winner who spent the last years of his life battling depression, alcoholism, and allegedly abusing his wife.

Jack's mother never questioned him about hockey again.

Uncle Mac invoked the spirit of his brother-in-law Nick Mandrak. "Mandrak the Magician," as he was affectionately referred to around the WIHL, was almost freakish in his six-foot-four height on the ice in the fifties as a goaltender for the Spokane Chiefs. He was getting looks from three NHL teams when a nagging rotator-cuff injury put a stop to that view. It wasn't exactly the shoulder but the surgery to fix it that nearly paralyzed him.

"Jack," Uncle Mac angrily blurted out, "you have everything your uncle had…height, skating skill, lean body mass, plus so much more… You owe it to Uncle Nick to stick it out. You know what Leo Geoffrion said about you in his scouting reports—there's never been a player out of B.C. with so high a hockey IQ. You've got to understand what that means." Mac seemed crestfallen, betrayed beyond words at Jack's decision. Beyond words it was, as Mac, walking out the door, put his head down as if he had lost the mate of his life.

Jack, following him, pleaded in his ever-placating tone, "Mac, I'll be back…I just felt I owed it to Uncle Nick, my dad, Mom, and everybody else to be the first one in the family to graduate from university…"

The clouds were darkening, and incoming fast eastwardly over the ocean toward the Vancouver shoreline. Mac, left hand on his car door, picked up his head, staring straight at Jack with a dagger-like squint, saying nothing. While the pain of Uncle Mac's look left Jack by the next day, the bone-deep memory of his stare did not.

Off Jack went, with the blessings of his coach, not entirely of his family, to finish university back East at McGill. Heading East, Jack felt that the only life he'd known was all behind him. It wasn't just Greater Vancouver. Waking up his first day in his Peel St. student apartment, Jack thought, "This is the first day I can remember that I am not even thinking of the ice, conditioning, or training regimen." He felt that what seemed like a life, a value system of hockey 24/7, was behind him.

Montreal was good for Jack. Montreal was the Louvre Museum of his life. It allowed him to peer into things so very foreign to him. People sitting down in cafés, sipping espressos in a manner that made it seem like he was watching slow-motion stills. The blur that now crossed before his eyes was not a high-velocity moving ice puck, but people interacting in their sundry routine manners. This was a student's life in Montreal in the 1970s. The seventy-five-cent meals of pea soup and French bread that as a university student he seemed to subsist on. Every once in a while, he and his newfound struggling student friends would get together and chip in for several dishes of "poutine." Eating this delicious dish of French fries, cheese curds, and gravy would fill you up for days. But it was the Montreal bakery bread from Mamie Clafoutis that was unforgettable. The bread was in itself remarkable…the smell…the grainy wholesome taste, still in his memory.

He studied well, volunteered at the St. Valliers' Juvenile Center, and took in all the museums a student had time to visit. His particular favorite was the McCord Museum, as he knew any discussion of it and its dedication to Canadian history would play well back home, especially with Uncle Mac. He needed that to bring home and diminish the excruciating interminable question "When are you going to return to the ice?" Jack had now long decided the up-and-down world of hockey that he had played in for the past twenty years of his life was behind him. His family felt there was something else that stood in the way of his pursuing his love of hockey. Hard as it was for Jack to put aside his passion for the game, it was harder for his family. When he came home for the summer, the family just assumed Jack would get back to training both for and on the ice.

When he announced he would not be playing for the Rockets, or any other team for that matter, Uncle Mac was the first one to remind him of the *Vancouver Sun* article that touted him as "the personified rebirth of British Columbia's hockey dominance." Jack proceeded to tell the family, "Somebody else is going to have to live up to that false prediction."

When Jack booked his second flight in two months back to Montreal, Uncle Mac was the first to say, "For a guy who complained about the high humidity in the Eastern provinces... you seem to want to go back there pretty much!"

There WAS something else Jack wanted back. "It" was actually a someone.

Her name was Morgan "Marbry" Wellington.

Jack met Marbry his second semester at McGill. She was majoring in speech pathology and they took a multi-departmental crossover communications course together. He never forgot the day she walked into class in what seemed like the most sensuous black dress a woman could ever wear. Jack wouldn't know Diane von Fürstenberg from nuclear fusion, but viewing Marbry in that dress set off the atomic particles in his DNA. He was intrigued by her sense of style, even the way she sat in class; she was a world apart from the "puck bunnies" that framed Jack's ideal of attractive females. He was certain she didn't notice him.

One day the professor suggested the class attend the Sherbrooke Speech Seminar over the weekend, an off-campus event featuring journalists and lecturers from the communications field. Walking out of class, this woman, whom he had tried not to stare at for two weeks straight, turned and looked his way. His heart racing, Jack contemplated, "Did she smile at me?" His thigh burnt, as he had just knocked into the last desk coming out of the classroom.

"Oh, are you all right?"

Jack, immediately intrigued by her apparent French accent, answered, "Yeah, ridiculous of me."

She continued, "I don't know about you, but I had a whole weekend planned. I guess if we want the grade we have to go to this seminar one of the days."

Stumbling over his words now, Jack offered, "Yes, I guess… What day was the seminar?"

"Oh, I see you're enthralled with the class as well?"

Gathering himself, Jack replied, "Saturday, I'm planning to attend Saturday… Can I meet you there?"

"Better yet, let's meet at the Chambois Café…it's my favorite place in this part of the city for French pastries and espresso… By the way, my name is Marbry."

The name sounded as sensuous as the woman he was looking at.

Jack didn't remember much about what was said at the seminar; rather, he was fixated on the meticulous note-taking by Marbry. From then on in, his time at McGill was with her. His "billet" now had become every hour he could be with her. From the way she took notes to her dimpled smile to her alluring voice that could whisper "Je t'aime…moi non plus" more seductively than Brigitte Bardot could sing it, Jack was smitten. As if that were not enough, their first dinner together, she asked, "What books have you been reading?"

Her family, the Wellingtons of LaSalle, Quebec, was a prominent family whose comfortable lifestyle was rooted in the masquerade and carnival costume business. Marbry was the second oldest of four of Walter and Millicent Wellington. The family had English ancestry on the father's side, and French on Millicent's side. Both languages were spoken and mastered at home. Before McGill, Marbry had been educated at the Sacred Heart of Montreal School.

She was the second Catholic girl he had dated; Susan Reynolds from back home, the first, was devotedly Catholic. Susan was also what Preston called "too hot to handle for Jack." Always looking for some older-brother inspiration from "Pres," Jack most often received just the very opposite. "I can't believe my younger brother thinks he can manage those cup sizes." Jack had deep respect for Susan, but chemistry was not in the cards for them. He wanted to stay close to her, but she declined when he asked her to go skinny-dipping one night at Lions Gate Park, telling him, "That's totally perverse, not to mention it's against my religion." When he responded, "How else will we get to know the true ins and outs of each other?" she demanded that he drive her home. Her point was driven home and so was she! It was therefore Jack's unbridled assumption that all Catholic girls were equally chaste and formally frigid.

However, Jack was soon to come to the realization that Susan's rule of Catholicism was not shared by Marbry. Perhaps there was more than Marbry's embellished French accent that intrigued Jack. Before the relationship was barely a month old, the relationship was, as Marbry put it in her elegant manner, "consummated" under the fir trees…a stone's throw from the beach-volleyball players at the Parc Jean-Drapeau. Marbry's allure was her dignified external refinement belying her internal passionate rapture. The sexy raspiness about her voice and movements mesmerized Jack. He was taken in by her sheer cosmopolitan sophistication combined with her total naiveté about "men's things."

"Jack, I always wondered...when do the hockey players know when to stop skating in the game?" Marbry quizzed him one day as they stepped off the Metro at the Place-des-Arts, the blue of the brick walls sharpening the beauty of her radiant blue eyes. With questions like that, whatever cosmos she came from, how could it really be Canada?

Marbry was Jack's guide into a new world he thought he was missing, and he very much was. She thought it cute in the manner of a child going to the zoo for the first time how Jack marveled at the "amazing amount of art galleries on Saint-Paul Street." She brought him to the site of where "Montreal Expo 67" took place, where the movie *Quintet* was being filmed.

"Paul Newman reminds me of you, Jack...I love his quiet intensity."

Marbry's most favorite movie was **Un Homme et une Femme**. "Jack, you would know it as *A Man and a Woman*."

"I would?"

"Oh, Jack, I have seen it three times. We must see it together... it is sooo romantic." When they did finally see it, Marbry cried after the first ten minutes; Jack fell asleep.

After several weeks of "courtship," as Marbry always put it, Jack was invited to Marbry's family house for dinner. This occasion, or any event at the Wellingtons', was no simple affair!

"Mother and Wellington would love to meet you."

"Wellington?" Jack could never get over how Marbry never could refer to her father as just "Dad."

Walking in the spacious center hall, Jack quickly turned to his left and laid his eyes on two plush white divans, the kind he'd seen Pamela Anderson strewn across in a poster Preston had hanging up a long time ago.

"Jack, hello, are you with me?"

"I knew your house would be palatial, Marbs, but I never expected *Better Homes and Gardens.*"

Bringing Jack through the ample center hall colonial, Marbry coyly remarked, "I take it that's a compliment...or were you expecting something more Western rustic? C'mon, Wellington and Millicent are waiting for us."

It was tacitly understood that Walter Wellington did not go by "Wally," and Millicent would certainly have some sort of heart failure had she been referred to simply as "Milly."

Mrs. Wellington floated around babbling incessantly. "Do take some of our delicious Brie, please, Jack...have you been to France...you ought to try the Merlot...it goes with the Brie, you know."

There was an unusual array of dinner guests that evening. "Marbs, sorry, but I thought, well, you know, it was just your parents and us."

"Jack, you'll just adore my family...if you can put up with them. The only one you won't get to meet is my younger brother, Addison, who is away at boarding school in the States... It's too bad, he lives for sport and knows hockey well...I think he's heard of you."

"Where does he board?"

"Well, he was at CPI right here in Montreal, but he's not exactly the best student. Wellington had some good connections down at Kent, so last year, much to the chagrin of my mother, off went Addison to Connecticut."

Her spectacular blue eyes zeroing right into Jack, Marbry mused, "There shall be plenty of time to meet him, Jack, right, plenty of time?" Plenty of time with Marbry only gave Jack a sense of utter placidity.

Jack, taking a "Theatre and the Arts Appreciation" course for non-drama majors at McGill, mused on how the family seemed to be channeling a Federico Fellini film. In that class he learned about Fellini's satire of the hedonistic upper class. Here he lay, witness to a living diorama of dilettantes. Her sister, Christiana, who had a face of indecent exposure written all over it, seemed to be a tad over-welcoming, especially when he could not miss hearing her whisper to Marbry, "He's got a great ass, Marbry." Then there were Christiana's husband, Chester, who seemed to be a lost soul in the far corner, stuffing his face with wheat crackers and cheddar cheese; Mr. Crick, the family accountant, who didn't mutter a word the whole evening; Marbry's mother's brother, Trent, whose Brooks Brothers button-down polished shirt, tie, and haircut couldn't belie a certain licentious half-restrained grin; a couple who were introduced as "Mr. Wellington's business partners, the Randis"; Celeste, Mrs. Wellington's "walking partner and best friend"; and a woman looking like she'd lived more than a century bespectacled in jewelry, large jewelry for a petite woman, and haute couture of purple, identified as "Cousin Tina." Cousin Tina was in fact ninety-five, and her deceased husband, Harrington, was a scion of a Halifax shipping company.

The most welcoming family member was Marbry's gay brother, Cooper. In a few short minutes, Jack learned more about Cooper than anybody else present.

"Jack, are you a Margaret Thatcher fan?"

"Well, honestly, I haven't given it much thought," Jack responded.

"Well, I just adore her sincerity and candor…you know they say she once scolded Pierre for 'being obnoxious and acting like a naughty schoolboy'!"

Jack momentarily pondered who Pierre might be, and quickly Marbry came to the rescue, allowing Jack to save face. "Yes, that was when Trudeau criticized the American president Reagan."

"Yes, I always loved her spunk," Jack roared, noticeably winning an ally with at least one family member.

Cooper, with his palm extending forever southward, told Jack, "Anytime you want to talk, Jack, I'm here… I'll give you the unadulterated truth AS ONLY a family black sheep can!"

"Stop trying to make a pass at Jack, Cooper. He's here with me."

"Oh, hush, Morgan. I'm still your very big brother!"

"Yes, and still the only person who calls me by that vile name Morgan."

"A little brotherly advice, Morgan, always remember who YOU are!"

Looking refreshingly removed from this crowd, with a gregarious face and equally friendly disposition, was their parish priest, Father "Ed."

It was a "proper Quebec crowd," if there ever was one, but, taking a look at Marbry's highbrow parents, Jack considered Marbry's genetic connection and pondered if Millicent and Walter were equally rapturous behind closed doors! It took him to the end of the evening to figure out that Mrs. Wellington's repetitive chorus of "Oh, Well" was not an uncorked interjection, but a direct address to her husband, Wellington. She, and only she, referred to the staid, silent man sitting at the head of the table as "Well."

Jack felt he was immediately being dissected as if he were a frog in the university lab. Christiana found her way to Jack, and felt compelled to attempt to make him even more uncomfortable.

"I'm intrigued with you, Mr. McKenna...usually Marbry dates older men, professors, society people, and the like."

Jack took it upon himself to use humor, something that seemed lost on this apparent dilettante. "Marbry didn't tell you... I am from Vancouver's high society...my family regularly climbs in the Bugaboos."

"Fascinating ...we might have a bugaboo with you," Christiana retorted, feigning a rueful frown across her pronounced forehead, accented by a skin leathered beyond her years.

Looking over through a masterful winkling of eyebrows that seemed borrowed from a royal herd of sheep, Millicent inquired, "What is it you do, Jack, and what will you be doing after graduation...Marbry said you spent a lot of time golfing in the past?"

"Mother! Please? Hockey!" Marbry chimed.

"Oh, of course...games all the same...games, games, games." Jack had already observed that one bottle of Chardonnay mysteriously emptied in front of Millicent and her relentless chatter, so he could not be offended. "We love games as well... Oh, Well...let's start playing a little game of charades...shall we?" The alcohol-induced detour of her original question gave Jack an unintended pass at answering it. Thus, Jack mused, his question was answered. After all, the family made its fortune on masquerade costumes, so it was easy to see the guise in their overcharged formality.

The charade game took place, and as taciturn as Mr. Crick remained, Celeste would take over the evening in her bombastic, bluestocking manner.

"Remember, all, I went to Vassar…so naturally this comes easy to me," Celeste cattily called out.

"What is Vassar?" Jack naively inquired.

Choking on her chocolate mousse, she replied, "Why, my god, oh dear, hmrmm, you never heard of Vassar? Well, it would be hard to describe."

"Good going, Jack. Never in her life had Celeste been so unintentionally brought down a peg," Marbry later quipped.

Seemingly out of place in this near-Fellini-esque scene was the priest. Although, as Jack was later to find out, having him present was the extent of the Wellingtons' active Catholicism, Father Edmonds seemed like a grounded human being to Jack. When Jack informed him he was not Catholic, asking, "Should I call you Father?" Edmonds fired back, "If you do, I won't answer. Call me Ed!"

Before he went back to BC, Jack felt he would like to get together with Father Ed, as he seemed not only "sincerely spiritual," and humbly brilliant, but the most interesting person at the table. Father Ed could discuss Pierre Trudeau's "reason before passion" motto with just the same ease as he could the legacy of the Montreal Canadians.

"My family's living, breathing token of 'We ARE Big Catholics'!" Marbry laughed to Jack.

"What's that supposed to mean? He seems like a genuine man," Jack retorted.

"Oh, HE is, but nobody else here, as you might have noticed, is! My parents think their Catholicism is measured by how much they donate, in their name, to be etched in the pews of the cathedral, and how often they have a priest like Father Ed to dinner, as if by sheer invitation alone they would be absolved from all their sins."

"What does it mean to you, Marbry?"

"What does what mean? Being Catholic?"

"I was always brought up to be leery of you guys."

"Leery of Catholics…why, Jack?"

"Well, as my uncle Mac always said…the Catholics are interested in only three things…real estate, worshipping their statues, and getting contributions."

"Jack, that is so unfair…are you proud of your family's bigotry?"

"No, that's why I asked you what it means to you… Well, what does it mean to you?"

"Jack, can we have this conversation at another time…it is getting very morbid."

"Okay."

"More importantly, what did you think of my family… absolutely adorable, aren't they?"

"Your dad isn't much for words…he seems like a man with a lot on his mind."

"That's just a reflection of his not trusting anyone," Marbry said calmly, but almost too assuredly.

"Why not?"

"C'mon, Jack, that's easy to figure out, he doesn't trust himself. Actually when I was real little I remember him as being the joy of every holiday, the festival within a festival, but then the THING happened when I was nine or ten, and quite frankly he has never been the same."

"What was the 'thing'?" Jack asked.

"It's something we really don't speak about, Jack!"

"Okay, what was it, an extramarital affair?"

"…No, that came later, along with everything else Mother ignores."

"Okay, Marbry…was he pictured with sheep…?"

"Jack, don't speak in your crude hockey jocularity…it was much more complicated."

"Can I hear about it…in case the 'thing' ever affects our relationship?" Jack barked.

"Okay…you love to dig things out of me, don't you, love? In the mid-sixties there was talk about a World's Fair in Montreal… my father was one of the prominent businessmen in the city, in the province, who initially thought it was not a good idea… our transportation centers and roads would be overwhelmed, was his thinking. Meeting with several people in business and politics, my father voiced his opinion. For some reason, Russia, which was originally going to host this World's Fair, pulled out and now Expo 67 was the province of the Quebec province, to be held in our fair city of Montreal. There was a management group formulated for this…and naturally most people thought my father would be chosen; he was a tremendous civic leader at the time. He was not.

"It seemed for originally giving some of his honest input, he was shut out. He was close to virtually all the men in this group. It was an impressive group; they were called 'Les Durs… the tough guys.' They created and managed everything around Expo 67, with the help, I might add, of Walter Wellington. The only thing was, they were all given credit…my father was given not even a thank you from his 'friends' in the end. The final straw and insult was when ten of the men considered so tough and dutiful and patriotic were honored by our government as recipients of the Order of Canada... Father was not even invited to the ceremony."

"Oh," Jack sheepishly commented, an ounce of sympathy expressed toward this staid-looking man who happened to be the father of the girl of his dreams.

"As repulsed as I am to say this, Jack," Marbry concluded, "that was the last time Father did something noble for anybody."

"Well, your mother is quite a personality...she never stopped talking, yet there was a certain welcoming warmth in her voice," Jack said as the two took a taxi back to campus.

For a long minute, there was palpable quiet as the taxi whisked down St. Catherine's St., Marbry staring away from Jack. Fixated on the chaotic blur of the hectic city they were whizzing by, Marbry said softly, but quite firmly, "Oh, yes, but she's the woman I hope I never turn out to be." That chilling comment was never forgotten by Jack.

"We are going over to an over-twenty-one bar on Rue Harris."

"Well, just how is a nineteen-year-old youngster like you going to get in, Marbs?"

"Don't worry about that." She showed Jack a perfectly made fake ID card. "My friend Clive is a master of this artistry."

"Who's Clive?"

"Just a guy around campus who helps us college kids get in places we want to."

The months and semesters seemingly closed in and the circuitous route to the end of Jack's formal education came to a close. There was little time to celebrate. Jack knew he had to return home for employment, and he wanted to maximize his time with Marbry, as the two would be apart indefinitely. Before he went back, Marbry's uncle, Trent, offered the two a weekend away at his Northern Ontario "getaway."

Trent's background was sketchy, but two things were abundantly clear: Trent a) was rich and b) lacked a moral compass. He'd apparently lost his job in the Chicago Mercantile Exchange and ventured back up north to "make a killing," as he would put it, selling used American Chryslers in the provinces. The forty-something-year-old lothario confided to Jack, "You can take my niece up there, and don't feel shy—I had more than my share of young babes up there screaming in ecstasy." The sentiment repulsed Jack, but the convenience of his free property did not.

"Jack, Mother is letting us borrow her Volvo…and best of all, it has a cassette player. I want you to hear my favorite song, 'D'amour ou D'amitié'…'Of Love or of Friendship.' It's so romantic, Jack…like us…and it's sung by a Quebec girl, Celine Dion…I adore it."

Hearing Marbry sing the song lifted Jack the way the tall red cedars alongside the highway did. Marbry would put her hand on Jack's shoulder and emphasize the words "Moi je l'aime et je peux lui offrir ma vie."

"What does that mean, Marbs?"

In the most seductive voice that Jack could take and still stay on the road, Marbry whispered, "I'll tell you tonight."

Arriving on the property after the three-hour drive and what seemed an interminable stretch on a narrow dirt road from the highway to the cabin, Jack and Marbry were surprised to find two cars parked in front of the property. After all, Trent had told Marbry the key would be found in the red flowerbox in the wooden tool shed by the shovels, hoes, and trowels. As they went up the creaky steps, Jack's and Marbry's ears were punctured by the Freddie Mercury music blaring from a turntable inside the door left ajar. Surprisingly, they heard multiple voices coming from the kitchen. Sure enough, it was Uncle Trent, entertaining three women and one perplexed-looking man. Perhaps he, too, had been promised a "weekend of privacy and solitude."

Trent, feigning surprise, announced, "Oh, I thought it was next weekend you two were coming up." Trent made some cursory introductions, and vanished with the man and two of the women. Marbry went upstairs to change and Jack was left with "Monique." Monique's French accent seemed to get thicker as she spoke. When Marbry came down, Monique was in the middle of explaining her film-directing career, which encompassed all forms of "the cinema verité," as she haughtily put it. She claimed to know Marbry's family well, which was odd, as Marbry knew little or nothing of her. Marbry and Jack went up to "retire," and Monique stared pointedly at both of them, with a look that could only be described as "expecting an invitation from them."

The night was spectacular. Marbry and Jack made love in the way that seemed all too special for normal beings. Whispering again, "Moi je l'aime et je peux lui offrir ma vie…" she told him, "It means, Jack, I love him and I could offer him my life."

In the morning, the smell of Belgian waffles woke Jack up from his splendid slumber. Jack washed first and went downstairs expecting to see all five whom they had unexpectedly walked in on the night before. It was only Monique, in the kitchen alone, clad in a stark blue bikini, stirring batter and staring blankly at Jack.

Marbry followed, asking, "Where is my uncle?"

To which Monique answered in a whisper-like tone, "Oh, they left sometime last night."

"Did my uncle leave a note?"

"Oh, no," Monique answered, "you should know Trent is a man of few words."

The appearance of Trent and company along with the disappearance of Trent and company was as strange as the fact that Monique, whoever she was, stayed the length of the time Marbry and Jack did. When they were leaving Sunday, she finally put on something over her blue bikini.

Despite that cryptic situation, the weekend went very well. Driving back to Montreal, Jack thought nothing but how much he loved Marbry. She seemed quiet. He assumed she was in the same state of nirvana he was, when all of a sudden she announced, "You would never guess he's a father of four!"

"Who?"

"My uncle Trent!"

"Whaaat…wait a minute, he was with the same woman for four children?"

"Yes, Jack."

"So was he…was he…actually married?"

"Yes."

Jack nearly drove into the evergreens along Highway 117, skidding to a halt.

"Jack, what are you doing?"

"Okay, Marbry, why the mystery? You never told me that!"

"Well, it's not something my family talks about."

"Apparently not, but you make it like it is cloak-and-dagger… Lots of people are divorced…and quite frankly, I'm not surprised that he was married so much as that he stayed with a woman long enough to have children, and four children to boot!"

"Drive, Jack, I don't want to talk about this."

"Okay."

The two stayed silent as the countryside and Jack's thoughts became less dense.

The spires of the Cathedral of Saint-Jerome were in sight when Marbry finally shouted out, "It was a tragedy, Jack, and my family does not like to dwell on tragedy."

"Okay, Marbry, I'm sorry…let's talk about the great lake we swam in nude together yesterday."

"No, you need to know…it might change your opinion of Uncle Trent…because of what he suffered. Two years ago, Trent and some of his work friends rented a getaway weekend at the Eaglewood Resort. It was a great weekend for the wives, the kids, the husbands. Sunday night, the men finished a card game later than they wanted…there was a lot of drinking. Helene, his wife, insisted on driving home. Driving north on 290, Helene claimed to have been swiped by a driver…"

"What do you mean 'claimed to have been'?"

"Well, I should say she was…they did find hours later a car and driver crashed into a tree with the body paint of their Chrysler on it. Anyway, Helene turned a three-sixty on the highway, another car hit her right side…the side their youngest daughter, Ernestine, was sitting in… She was dead on arrival at St. Mary's and Elizabeth's. Trent too was in a coma two days in the hospital; miraculously he survived, Jack… Jack, think of how when he came to, they told him he had lost his youngest child… think of how devastated any man would be… When he went home, Jack, he was so upset, he was a little physically unsure of himself with Helene."

"What do you mean 'he was a little physically unsure of himself'?"

"Well, he hurt Helene."

"You mean he hit her?"

"Yes, Jack…but understand what he went through. Neighbors had been coming by to bring meals, but unfortunately they saw that…the police arrived and Trent was arrested for assault and battery… Helene took the children and he lost all custodial rights.

"The wake was so sad and horrible… Mother was so upset at the wake that she was devoid of emotion. The night before the wake she called my cousin Roger, an RCMP, to tell him the terrible news, and she said, 'Just make sure your uniform looks bright and prominent for the wake'…she even reprimanded me for crying…' How could you cry? We are Wellingtons and we don't cry for ourselves.' Oh, Jack, I hope you understand how very terrible it was and is for poor Trent."

"Well, he suffered all right," Jack thought to himself. But he hadn't changed his opinion of Trent.

Bennett

WITH JACK RETURNING TO BRITISH Columbia, he pursued his interest in juvenile reform. His interest in that stemmed from the metamorphosis that he'd witnessed in his best friend from his youth, Bennett Malley. At twelve, Malley lost his dad, and in the interim, a bit of his way. Witnessing his father die a slow death due to pancreatic cancer, Bennett became angry and energetically destructive. Jack always liked to tell the almost clichéd story of his close friend "hanging around with the proverbial wrong crowd; trouble always seemed to follow Bennett." What finally put him in trouble with the law was not his spray can that he vandalized the best of Pemberton Heights to Windsor Park with, but what Jack always saw as a "noble act of violence."

Bennett, a strong young man, and perhaps the most athletic of all of Jack's childhood friends, once single-handedly overturned his neighbor's coveted 1973 Satellite Sebring that the neighbor kept like a shrine in his driveway. It might be said that he had good reason to. With his mother two years widowed, the neighbor had apparently told her one cloudy day as she brought in her groceries, "Margie, at this point, don't you think you need a little something up your engine?" It wasn't the overturned classic automobile that landed Bennett in the juvenile reform system, but his punch that downed McKinley, the neighbor, putting him in the hospital for three days. He was decent enough to ask not to be placed "in the same ward where Nurse McKenna is."

"Aside from Bennett's signature work as a Marlboro-chain-smoking vandal at thirteen, he had the biggest heart of anybody I ever met," Jack would say when telling the story about his life's best friend to Marbry.

Always speaking of Bennett in a near-reverential tone puzzled Marbry. "I don't get it, Jack, wasn't he an adolescent delinquent?"

Jack would immediately reply, "A one-time unruly protector… he spent a little time in a juvie, but look how he turned out!"

Jack was always impressed with the fact that due to steely juvenile reformers in Western Canada, Bennett went from a possible youthful incarceration to a peaceful and productive adulthood. By the time he was fifteen, he was without a cigarette and running for the Stanley Park Striders. He eventually became one of the fastest mid-distance runners in Western Canada. When America's legendary Villanova track and field coach, Jumbo Elliott, started recruiting the great Canadian Athletics athletes the likes of Dean Childs and Glenn Bogue, he offered Bennett a full scholarship as well.

Jack, innately a perpetual idealist, and motivated by Bennett, felt that sport could work best for societal reform. His college thesis was on the "Effectiveness of Sport on Behavior Modification." He witnessed how Canada inaugurated its national hockey "Program of Excellence" for under-seventeen-year-olds in 1981. This nationally supported government program to find, train, and hone the country's best young players led to Canada winning the World Junior Gold Medal in 1982, their first World Junior title ever. He recalled the story of how when the Canadian Junior team won the gold medal, there was no copy of the Canadian national anthem in the Rochester, Minnesota, arena, and so the team sang, memorably, the national anthem themselves. He felt that if given a supported chance, young juveniles in trouble with the law could thus gain a sense of belonging with the right nationally funded program. His brain, firing on all cylinders, was figuring how he could simultaneously bring meaning to his life, help to his country that he loved, and honor to his family name, once so revered in Canada.

For meeting for drinks in Vancouver, there was only one place to go that combined history, hockey, memories, and great beer. It was the downtown St. Regis. The hotel actually sponsored a team in the forties in the Pacific Coast Hockey League.

Over some chilled Labatts at the St. Regis, Jack told Bennett, "There's a developing juvenile reform program in the States, in Southern Washington, called JANUS… They have the right thing going…but I can take my concept further."

"What's that?"

"Bennett…think of how sports directed you the right way!"

"Oh, I forgot…it was sports, was it, eh?!" Bennett answered, amused.

With the fervor of a candidate on a political stump speech, Jack demanded, "Young boys need sports, and they need the RIGHT men directing them in that… Hockey was good to me. I've done the playing…and I'm done with that…but I'm not done using that background for the right thing!"

Acquired Notions

JACK ALWAYS BELIEVED HE COULD mine support from an odd quarry.

As troubled as his uncle was with his leaving the game, Jack believed he secretly would support him down the road in this endeavor. Jack knew well the stubbornness that was in Uncle Mac's DNA, and how he defined the "test and rigors of manhood."

Yes, "the test and rigors of manhood"—Jack had heard that all too many times. When Jack was seven, Uncle Mac decided "it was time for Jack and Preston to taste the great outdoors and sip into the Skeena." Uncle Mac was going to take Jack and Preston on one of his legendary fishing trips in Northern British Columbia. A day before the scheduled trip, Preston came down with a strange stomach virus and, of course, Marguerite would not let him go on the trip. For Mac, you never postponed or canceled one of these trips. So off went Mac, one of his old wartime buddies, Chris Johnstone, and Johnstone's grandson, Philippe, two years older than Jack, flying deep into the pristine waters of Northern British Columbia for what was to be an adventurous fishing expedition.

The first night of the trip, Jack had his first experience of seeing men covet bottles of beer in the way he only knew from coveting his stuffed animals himself. Three days into the trip the boys woke up in the lodge with nobody and nothing but their fishing equipment left with them. Jack immediately felt assured that his uncle and his friend were just trudging about the thick woods to hunt some food. Philippe, reading the reality of the situation better as a nine-year-old boy, seemed to panic that his grandfather would not be back too soon, if at all.

"Grandpa J…I just know he won't be back."

The boy was almost right, as the two adults did not show up for hours. Jack spent the better part of the day coming up with games to keep Philippe's mind off the adult's unannounced disappearance.

"Let's play a word game, and I'll be sure to give you hints."

Intermittently Philippe cried and shook like the small Cessna plane that took them to the wilderness, continuing, "What do we do if they don't come back?"

At nightfall, the men arrived, smelling strangely and laughing vigorously. Simultaneously, they announced to a confused Jack and a hysterical Philippe, "Well, congratulations, boys, you survived… You are now men."

However, with Philippe still visibly traumatized, Grandpa J didn't hesitate to insult Philippe.

"Oh, stop being a big pussy."

This only served to make the broken boy shake more. At seven years old, Jack had been anointed into the world of misguided manhood.

They arrived back home with seven of the biggest steelhead Jack would ever see in his life and some great-looking pictures of the mountains and streams that Johnstone took on his Polaroid, yet Jack had no recollection of the five days on the trip except that one long day consoling Philippe. In a warped way he always felt that, however unforgettably frightening the experience was not only for Philippe, but for him as well, he at least "passed the test of manhood" Uncle Mac had placed upon him. That would be a feeling he personally found perverse and one that he purposely kept to himself.

He saw Philippe once in the next six years. He was surprised when the boy seemed to avoid him at one of Uncle Mac's "Canada Day" barbecues. Not too long after that, Jack felt the first tremors of his teenage years when, one day after hockey practice, his mother asked him if he remembered "the boy who went on Uncle Mac's fly-fishing expedition with you?"

Jack, who'd never let on the details of that trip to his mother, who, he felt, had been burdened enough by the disparities of life, said, "Yes, of course."

"Well, Jack, remember him in your prayers. God took him from his family today." Philippe Johnstone had died of a drug overdose at the age of sixteen.

Despite the strangely overdramatic send-off Uncle Mac had given Jack the last time the two saw each other, Jack still sought his uncle's approval for his latest undertaking.

"A far-fetched fantasy," Uncle Mac roared one night, "but a noble one, eh…you can still do some good for your country, in the manner that's written in your family's genes."

Constructing such support, and doing it as a career, became Jack's goal. He knew he had the support of his former hockey cronies, and most certainly the vast network of his uncle, not just in hockey but also in Canadian sport. A goal in place, some support to realize it, Jack told Bennett, "I know I can put this together, I feel it; life right now seems like a dream…and if I don't, you'll have my back like Semenko had Gretsky's," referring to the loyal, protective tough-guy Oiler's teammate of the "Great One."

Due to visit Marbry back East in a few weeks, Jack received a call very early one morning from her. She asked him if he could come back East sooner than he had planned. He longed for Marbry. She could have asked him to meet in Kamloops that afternoon and Jack would have turned the world upside down to comply.

"It sounds urgent, Marbs... I'll get a plane to Dorval this weekend."

"Could you make it next weekend, Jack? Mother and Wellington are down in New York staying at the Plaza...Mother loves Raul Julia, Wellington loves Broadway, and they have tickets for the play *Nine* and won't be back until next Wednesday."

Was something wrong with her parents' health? Jack wondered...but no, why would they be traveling? The following week Jack flew back and reflected indulgently on time spent with Marbry. He thought of kissing the back of her neck, massaging her shocking waves of curly hair, caressing what he referred to as her "Montreal snow-white skin."

Jack assumed that meeting Marbry in the baggage-claim area would be a repeat of the first day of laying eyes on her in class. Rushing downstairs, he almost fell off the escalator.

One look in Marbry's eyes and he knew...she was pregnant.

"How far along?"

"Two months," Marbry answered. Her voice was vulnerable, but her azure blue eyes radiated with a sensuous fierceness.

This was the woman Jack loved. She, a very short time ago, seemed to have been dropped in his world from the cosmos. It had all seemed so right. "This, too, would be part of the natural order of celestial sequences," Jack murmured to himself.

"What did you say, Jack?"

Hugging her, he couldn't say a thing.

With Jack staying in one of the family guest rooms back in LaSalle, he asked Marbry if he could speak to her parents alone. Jack felt forever entwined with Marbry, like the English ivy on many of the old buildings back in B.C. His main worry was how she might be treated by her family. Marbry insisted that was not a good idea, and the very next day, the two broke the news over afternoon Brie and tea! Surprisingly enough, Millicent handled it well, but Walter sprang up from the leather sofa, harping, "Now that they made their bed, let them lie in it."

"Well, oh, Well, can't you come back and speak with your daughter at this time?" The vestibule door slammed, and off went Walter.

The cacophony of the cataclysmic closing of that door reverberated in Jack's psyche for what seemed like eternity, although it was merely milliseconds. Within hours, plans for a September wedding were made.

Later that evening, Walter came down and, speaking in a purposely loud voice to be heard behind closed doors, stated what could only be in his mind an acquiescence to the very notion of the ceremony. "Considering the disgrace of this deed for our family and all who are involved in our family, the wedding shall be small and in the ancillary chapel in the basement of the rectory."

Millicent held firm in her ground that the wedding would be in a church proper. Both Marbry and Jack heard what would be perhaps the first time Millicent ever stood up to Wellington. "My daughter will not be in the subterranean of anything."

That was the good news, as Jack felt this was a happy, albeit not perfect, occasion, and neither he nor Marbry wanted to be "hidden in disgrace in some obscure chapel." The wedding, however, ended up being held not in their local parish but in St. Patrick's Basilica downtown. Rather than ponder the location change, Jack saw only the hidden omen. Although he was not Catholic, he was Irish enough to see "the luck."

Jack finally got to meet Marbry's younger brother, Addison, albeit in an almost unusual manner. As Jack remained laden with thoughts on how and where his life was going to take him, in walked "Addie."

"Well, hello," the diminutive younger brother said earnestly, hand outstretched.

"Looks like due to the absence of a condom you're going to be part of the family?!"

Jack, hesitating to either punch this little freckled-faced wise guy straight in the eyes or hug him for breaking the tension thick as soup in the house, was relieved that Addie laughed.

"Well, don't fret; I for one am looking forward to a guy who will talk more than stocks and bonds and the latest company P&L Explained."

At the moment he felt he had a family ally, Marbry walked back in. "Jack, good you met Addie, but there is something else important for us to speak about."

The not-so-good news for Jack was that Marbry insisted that the child would have to be brought up Catholic. Jack knew this was not going to be welcomed news back in Delbrook! His family's Scottish-Presbyterian lineage would show its face not so much in Sunday church pews but in their provincial pride. Jack felt the only time religion took on any conversational substance in his house was when it involved an anti-Catholic fervor. Uncle Mac would ramble about how "the papists own all the prime real estate in B.C.," and how he "couldn't believe that one of Jack's teammates in Junior A play missed an important tournament for a Catholic cult ritual—a confirmation!"

Jack's mother would explain away her brother's Catholic bigotry by saying, "It was a Catholic boy from back East who stole the love of his life when he came back from the war." Nevertheless, Jack felt religion should be about coexistence, not division. He knew full well what religion his family shunned, but he did not know much about his own religion. After all, in Jack's family it was Uncle Mac who laid down the commandments, and in everything but religion, Mac always seemed to stand tall, dignified, even considerate.

This was going to be Marbry's and his life, not her family's and not his family's. He felt his love for Marbry was more than a needed glue for what he knew was not going to be a blissful bonding of two disparate families. Marbry reminded Jack how he admired Father Ed, and he would be the priest performing the ceremony, guiding him through the pre-cana. "Pre what?" chimed Jack…

"Oh yeah, that's another Catholic ritual you'll need to do," Marbry answered. Agnes Rouchard, one of Marbry's sorority sisters from Kappa Kappa Gamma at McGill, would be the maid of honor, and Bennett would be Jack's best man. Marguerite insisted that the "right and proper thing would be to have your brother Preston as your best man." Just when Bennett was going to concede what he called "the honor" to Jack's brother, Preston solved that conundrum by stating,

"I'm nobody's best man but my own." Now in his late twenties and living in the Northeast in the United States, Preston spoke words that were both literally and figuratively true. Preston was on his fourth job but now seemingly settled, teaching history and coaching hockey at a Massachusetts high school.

Bennett was thrilled with this latest honor. Both Bennett's life and his running life had been going well. He had run 3:41.2 in the 1500 meters, which was the converted-time equivalent of a sub-four-minute mile. He achieved his goal of representing Canada in international competition. A tear in his Achilles during a training session in Dublin brought him home and kept him off the Pan-Am games team that summer. Nevertheless, Team Canada requested he come with the team to Caracas "in a managerial and inspirational capacity." There, waiting for the opening ceremony, he met a beautiful American swimmer from Los Gatos, California, named Priscilla Caulkins.

Jack and Marbry's wedding reception was held at the University Club of Montreal, or "Le Club Universitaire de Montréal," as Marbry referred to it.

"Interesting how your dad pulled out all the stops, for a person who wanted to relegate us to the back of the cathedral, Marbs."

"Jack, Wellington doesn't hold back when a party is involved, and he can invite his old-world drinking buddies and his old-world women…besides…Mother had the last say here! Wellington wanted to have it up at their country club on Mont Tremblant, but Mother insisted this was 'her club.'"

"Wait, they belong to both clubs?"

"Yes, Mother prefers the University Club, for its better dining privileges."

"So both your parents golf? I didn't know that!"

"Jack, be serious, neither of them golf; the club accords them the prestige they need."

Bennett brought Priscilla to the wedding, and immediately Jack saw the spark in Bennett's eyes. Priscilla lit up a spark in most of the guests' eyes.

"Who's 'Helen of Troy' hanging with Bennett?" quipped Arne Rosenfeld. Rosenfeld had interned his second semester junior and senior year of Princeton with the Rockets. Not only was that a unique distinction for a "Tiger," but Arne also usually held the distinction of being truly the smartest guy in the room wherever he went, east or west.

"Oh, that's Bennett's main squeeze he met in Caracas— Priscilla," answered Jack.

"Priscilla? Seriously? What's Ben trying to channel, Elvis?" Rosenfeld chortled.

"Well, they certainly do look right together."

"That woman would make anyone look right together," snarled Arne.

It was not an easy thing to do for Arne, compliment. It was hard not to…the vanilla-white hardened Canadian and the tall, blonde, bronzed Californian—they indeed sparkled. Jon Lee, another friend of Jack's who'd made the trip back East, asked, "Did my ears hear correctly, did Arne actually just produce a compliment?!"

Freshly graduated from the Woodrow Wilson School of International Diplomacy at Princeton, Arne was indeed an intellectual, but a diplomat he was not! His senior thesis as a "Tiger" was entitled "Minor League Play/Major League Failure." It essentially was a treatise on how the management of the Rockets failed their team by not cultivating American banking (thus international) support and financing. He appeared to cultivate a little of the East Coast elitism in his days off Nassau St. Nevertheless, the Rocket players loved him. There was mutual good-natured ribbing between the rough-and-tumble men of hockey and the brilliant, bespectacled, fast-talking Jersey boy.

"Arne, you are in a desert of women out where you are, aren't you?"

"Say whaaat?"

"Yeah, I read Princeton women were voted the ugliest in the Ivy League," Charlie Moreau professed pointedly.

"Charlie, you wouldn't know Princeton, New Jersey, from Princeton down on the Tulameen."

"Well, I do know that I wouldn't be caught dead trying to find a woman in the Northeast U.S!"

"Oh really, why is that, Beau Brummel?"

These words drew in people amongst a chorus of laughter. "You're probably just talking about the women over forty...it's true, the winters are long, and they don't exercise as people do out West!"

"Hey, Jack, remember we played that exhibition game in Buffalo, New York?...I was telling you guys that I had never been to an arena where there are no women! Coach McC snapped back, 'Chuck, check that...look around, half the people in this arena ARE women, you just can't tell them apart!'"

"Maybe it's just upstate New York... but those women are rough," Charlie confirmed.

If Priscilla and Bennett looked right together, there was a couple that did not. It was Trent and a woman from the Deep South named Kendra.

"Jack, is that Marbry's uncle's daughter he is dancing with?"

"Nooo…that's his latest conquest… Yeah, she's half his age."

"Funny, when I came in, I thought he was the Old Man Wellington you told us about," Arne commented.

Jack's mom astutely commented to his cousin, Tom, "Everybody is talking about some other couple; I don't hear them talking about Jack and Marbry!"

The air of that truth was minimized, as the wedding day itself was a great one. Jack's closest friends from his school years and his hockey life, which were indeed the sum total of his youth, were present. Even Wellington seemed to get a kick out of Bennett, referring to him as "quite a pistol!"

Marbry, starting to show only to the staring eye, looked beautiful, but a mite uncomfortable. Jack NEVER looked so comfortable, his friends seemed to notice. Bill Bensen told Arne, "Jack told me last night 'I feel what Fitzgerald wrote about in *This Side of Paradise*…that we "slipped briskly into an intimacy from which we never recovered."'"

"I never knew he was romantic, or that he read Fitzgerald," Arne mused. "You know he was one of our own?"

"Fitzgerald was Jewish?"

"Bill, I meant he was a Princetonian."

"Well…some people can be changed by places…Montreal changed Jack, and I would say for the better."

Arne might have been right about that, but some people weren't changed by places in the least, and in those cases, it was also for the better. McKenna had always stayed in touch with his former Juniors teammate Bill "Billy B" Bensen. Bensen was not only a teammate of McKenna's, but also one of the youngest players at the time in the Canadian Juniors in the early eighties. Bensen utilized his six-foot-four height to intimidate his ice foes, but skated like a "five-foot-two whirlwind" according to a University of Saskatchewan coach. At the summer showcase camp in Kingston, Ontario, for the 1982 Canadian World Juniors team, Bensen was considered one of the top three desired players of the twenty-one that made the team out of the thirty-one to show up. One of the top players the coaches were counting on, Tony Tanto of the Oshawa Generals, was injured, and conventional wisdom might suggest that the coaches would be more aggressive in their selections, but just the opposite was the rule. The wisdom and prudence of the Canadian Junior coaches, painful in the short term, proved to be prescient in the long term. Bensen, who had survived a frightening concussion in a game against the Cornwall Royals the year before, was watched like a hawk. On the third day of the tryouts, Bensen went head over wall on a clean stick from Pierre Rioux, and was out for three minutes. When he came to, he knew he was out of the camp, and out of the game. He was the second of the three top hopes to be forced out. On that final day of the camp, "All-World" Juniors forward Brian Bellows was sent home, as he still couldn't move his separated shoulder. In late December, the final selected team boxed the Soviets out of a goal on Boxing Day in the raucous Winnipeg Arena, shutting them out 7–0 in what one Ontario sports writer called "Canada's Miracle on Ice."

Bensen would proudly tell how "the team went on to defeat the Czechs and win Canada's first World Junior Hockey title.

Every member of that team went on to play in the NHL, and as tight as they stayed together as a team, they forgot those who were almost there." At least this was the feeling of Bensen. Bensen always felt that his heart was "in the shape of a maple leaf," as he would tell people, and when the opportunity to represent his country at such a high stage came so close, and yet so far, Bensen seemed to lose a little nationalistic fervor. He had already become quite comfortable as a college student in the States. As brilliant as he was on the ice, he was a brilliant student at the Huxley School of Environmental Studies at Western Washington University.

Bensen had grown up in Kelowna, British Columbia, and as his hockey career was coming to a close, Kelowna was being granted a franchise team in the Western International Hockey League. The depression of his fleeting moment with stardom did not diminish his love for the game. Bensen and his dad, Werner, fervently followed the Kelowna team and its ultimate move to Spokane as the "Spokane Chiefs." Father and son would often travel around the Western cities and the Pacific Northwest to follow the team. Werner fell in love with the "inland empire" city of Spokane. One overcast summer day, Bensen's dad told Bill, "Your mother and I decided we are leaving the clouds and Catholics of Kelowna for some sun, Lutheran brotherhood, and U.S. citizenship." The move didn't surprise Bensen, Jr., but its immediacy did. Soon enough, Bensen regaled McKenna and his hockey brothers about the opportunities and the beauty that the U.S. Pacific Northwest had to offer. Jack listened, as he always did to Billy B, intently. Bensen was already enjoying credible success as an engineer having major stadiums and public venues around the West convert to green lighting alternatives.

Always forward-thinking and looking out for his friends, Bensen zealously told Jack at the reception about the progressive juvenile-reform movement currently taking place in Washington State.

"Jack…there is only one place now for you to live and follow that wide-eyed dream of yours… Your cousin lives in Oly and you can use his address while you get a job and get settled." Tom, Jack's first cousin, had no problem leaving Canada to go south. He was never interested in hockey, let alone sports. He was raised with a tad less patriotic zeal than Jack, and it wasn't an act of treason to live and work down in the States, as it might be considered with the McKennas. Tom was an academician always, and graduated with honors from Washington State University in Pullman. He was already a successful city planner in Olympia, Washington.

Of course Bensen stated this within earshot of the inebriated Tom, who steadfastly stuttered, "Yeah, Jack, it's about time you joined me in the States. You were awways like a big bro-other to me." Jack had no intention of moving his family in with Tom, but his address and contacts in Olympia were certainly things to take advantage of. "Remember, I know people in the capitol!" Tom, a zealous environmentalist, had worked hard to bring down the reign of Dixy Lee Ray as governor. "We supercharged her and her Puget Sound supertankers out of office…no easy task!"

Jack's mother, a "lover of the earth," as she would often identify herself, would keep the newspaper clippings of Tom's pro-environmental accomplishments. Tom was the first hero in the McKenna/Whately clan who didn't play hockey. Tom's contacts in the capitol city would be helpful for Jack to get started, and it would be good to have a family ally as well. For, as far as most of the McKennas were concerned, it was, as Bennett told him,

"You marrying Catholic and moving to the States…well, this is your second act of family treason… The first was putting away your shin guards and hockey stick… You might as well become an atheist and move to Moscow…Russia, not Idaho!"

The wedding was a feast of fun and frivolity. Everybody seemed to get along extremely well. Cooper approached Jack at the end of the night, three sheets to the wind, proclaiming, "This marriage could work well after all, Jack… Welcome to the family." Palm still extending forever southward, Cooper gave Jack a bear hug goodbye, whispering, "Again, feel free to talk whenever, and don't let Christiana prevent you from doing that!"

"Cooper," Jack asked, "speaking of Christiana, where was her husband, Chester?"

"My GOODNESS, Jack, did it already start, didn't anybody tell you…she dropped him like a hot potato!"

"Dropped him like a hot potato…do you mean separated from him?"

"Jack…their marriage is over, divorced and all, and Christiana's working on an annulment as we speak." Looking over at the bar, he commented, "Well, I guess after she stops drinking and flirting."

"Cooper, what did you mean 'did it already start?'"

"My family and their secrets, Jack. They love to keep things from one another—a learned trait, maybe acquired from our family business."

As foreboding as those words were, Jack couldn't consume himself with such gossip, whether true or not. He reveled in the joy of the day and his feeling that his friends and family were happy and behind the event. Uncle Mac, in his most complimentary manner, told Walter Wellington that evening, "You folks are not as bad as I figured Catholics to be!"

Hearing that, Bennett reminded Jack, "We can pick our friends, but not our families!"

Marbry and Jack would honeymoon in Bermuda, solidifying the placid world they were in. Unknown to them at the time, it would be a long time before they would be basking in clear blue seas and warm skies overhead.

Brave New World

JACK FIGURED OUT THAT THE most suitable place to live would be a city in Washington State close enough to what he was familiar with. Bellingham, Washington, less than an hour from Vancouver, was a beautifully unheralded city surrounded by a labyrinth of evergreens off the Puget Sound. After a week in Bermuda, Jack would fly with Marbry back to Montreal. Bennett and Jack then would drive Marbry's "special armoire" and belongings cross-country in Bennett's 1979 Volkswagen Vanagon. They even tied down Marbry's favorite bedroom mattress on the roof. Their plan was to take the Trans-Canadian Highway with one stop in Winnipeg, staying with one of Jack's former Rocket's teammates, Ray Clancy, who was coaching a top-notch Juniors A team there.

"Well, one thing is for sure, Jack, it's going to be a brave new world for you out there," Bennett said profoundly as he wished the new couple goodbye. The truth of Bennett's statement was in Jack's psyche…just buried under all the "to-dos" of immediacy since he'd landed in Montreal to discover and accept Marbry's news.

His hockey life was a billowing of routine, routine, routine, never having time to "stop and smell the roses along the way," until one day, and it was one day, as he liked to tell friends, he wanted it no more…thus changing the geography of both his life and his location.

A Bermudian honeymoon solidified the placid world they were in. Bennett's words echoed in Jack's head on the flight to Vancouver.

"Jack, did you speak to my uncle Trent at the reception?"

"Yes, together we surveyed who of all the chicks in the bridal party would be the easiest lay!"

"Jack, that's disgusting!"

"Yes, but that's Uncle Trent!"

"You just have something against him… He could be really helpful to us."

"Okay, after I nominate him for North American citizen of the year, how do I find him helpful?"

"Funny. I was hoping you would speak to each other… Trent is back in finance. He is working for an investment firm."

"What?" Jack asked incredulously.

"Yes, and you should know he already has some pretty prestigious customers lined up in your city of Vancouver!"

"You don't say? Okay, fill me in… How does a guy get kicked out of an industry, start selling used Chryslers, and then get back in the industry he was kicked out of?"

"You know the older gentleman who was dancing with my friend Gloria at the end of the night… He is a big wheel with Canadian Pacific Airlines."

"Oh, you mean Catastrophe Pacific…the shaky one?!"

"Jack, stop it, why are you so negative… We are going to take any good financial advice my uncle has to offer…and Jack, honestly, I think you are going to more than need it!"

Jack shook his head in his first conciliatory marital gesture. Jack would rather listen to Captain Smith of the *Titanic* on how to navigate icebergs safely than listen to Trent Doertz on any matters of anything.

"Magical!" Jack would tell Marbry about Bellingham, Washington. He convinced her that she would love the symmetry of the serene beauty enveloping the city and the location near to the very cosmopolitan cities of Vancouver and Seattle. The opposition he thought he might face for not only moving Marbry to the States but moving to a small city as well never arrived. It seemed that at that point Marbry's eyes met the passion in Jack's voice and she believed what he believed—that this was going to be a very settled move, let alone life.

They settled in an artsy area called Fairhaven. Jack's mother had a friend who was a professor at the nearby university, Western Washington, and recommended this area highly for a "young couple." Jack, landing the job with the State Department of Corrections, was going to be doing a lot of commuting, so it was important to him that the place would be safe, peaceful, and interesting mainly for Marbry, or so he told people.

The first night settled in, Jack had never felt so secure in his life. Marbry stared lovingly in his eyes as he kissed her from head to toe and she felt his body within hers, a breeze blowing in off the bay through their open window.

Marbry was still radiantly sensuous in her pregnancy. They always fit together so well in every sense of the phrase. His thoughts of love penetrating her psyche, her refined buttocks riding him lovingly, Jack caressing her elegant nipples endlessly, the imagery of her in her black dress in his first sighting of her doubling the ecstasy of feeling, loving, and sharing each other brought him to scream.

At the outset, it was clear that working for the state wasn't going to be the smooth cooperative venture he'd sought out. It didn't take long for Jack to realize his ideas, his experience at St. Valliers, and his hockey exploits meant little or nothing to anybody in the Department of Youth Corrections. Jack was on his own in a new job, a new country, and a new life.

Jack took an afternoon to go down to Olympia to have lunch with Tom.

"Tom, it just seems everything here is so politically chained and locked up…so much more than I ever expected."

"Jack, we all gambled that when Dixy Lee was voted out of her governor's office, there would be more of a reform-mindedness… not the case with this new administration. It almost seems more reactionary than hers!"

"Whatever came up with that outfit in Southern Washington, Jannet or something?"

"JANUS, and they are good people, but their model doesn't embrace sports for behavior modification."

"Tom, do you know down in California, at San Quentin State Prison, they have a baseball team that actually plays outside teams on prison grounds… I'm talking hardened criminals… murderers, and the like…and the rate of recidivism is near nil."

"No surprise there, Jack, anything is possible with Moonbeam as governor." "Well, maybe we should get some of Jerry Brown's beams up here!"

"Do you remember Uncle Mac's friend up in Vancouver who always would brag about his brother, who was some Bing

Crosby-type of priest back east in the U.S...and Uncle Mac would call him the "troubled boys' savior'?"

"Tom, do you mean the guy who had the school my mother used to threaten that she would send us to when we got in trouble?"

"Yes, don't you remember they were actually trying to get Bennett in there at one point?"

"Hard to believe, but yes, I remember that, but they couldn't because it was a school with some sort of Catholic religious affiliation for boys who were from one of the States back there!"

"You know the funny thing about that was it was Uncle Mac who was suggesting it...the ole Catholic bigot himself... Was he just trying to patronize his friend?"

"No, I think he actually met the priest himself and they both called each other Mac!"

"C'mon, Jack, Mac, despite some of his strange prejudices, was deep down the most socially conscious and caring guy we both knew. Remember hearing how he was one of the only prominent voices in the province expressing outrage about the exploitation of the Dionne quintuplets?!"

"Oh yeah...he felt that the country was going mad profiting off of those kids in a virtually publicly exposed incubator."

"Mac always holds fast to his principles, and I'm sure he recognizes and respects when he comes across another human who is equally vested in some sort of helping or standing up for some aspect of humans in need."

"Wow, this is wild...I really remember that guy now when he came to Vancouver...we thought he was Santa Claus."

"I wonder if he is still around with that school? High time you called your uncle."

"What do you mean by that?"

"I talked to him the other night and he said he hasn't heard from you in weeks…and, Jack, that's not good."

No, it wasn't; after all, it was Uncle Mac who told him, "Family always comes first, right ahead of ideals and principles." He'd reiterated that to Jack at the wedding, the last time Jack saw him.

Tom was always good for Jack. With Jack preoccupied with the realization of his dream, he could not let Marbry know he was struggling with the reality of its implementation.

Returning home that evening, Jack was greeted by Marbry with "How was saving the world today?"

"Okay, Marbs, you'll have to get a new line," Jack said. "Well, you look like you are ready…so I had better save this world fast before our child comes."

"I hope you didn't forget tonight is our last Lamaze class."

That was both great news and terrible news to Jack. He just couldn't bring himself to indulge in the joy that the other couples seemed to embrace in the class. He loved kissing Marbry's behemoth belly, and talking to the womb, but the public displays of passion for child he felt were beyond the palatable pale. It brought him back to memories of the dreadful pre-cana class they had attended religiously taught by a middle-aged French-Canadian couple back in Quebec. It was hard enough for both of them to embrace the couple's over-zealous spiritual perspective, but on the night of the fourth class, the discussion of "Sex in Marriage," the hosts, the Labartines, really seemed to step way out in a stratosphere that could only be described as, well, way out of character for them. Mrs. Labartine, who had previously come across as a mix of a monastic nun and Lady Woodrow Wilson, announced, "God deems that within marriage, anything GOES in the bedroom." Jack knew that night when Mrs. Labartine put the emphasis on the G in "GOES," it was going to be tough to, well, swallow. Mrs. Labartine left the invisible nun's habit he imagined her wearing that night and proceeded to tell in detail how "pleasant it is for her to go down on her husband…she just can't get enough of his hard rocket." The saving grace was when Marbry got up, saying she had "some strange stomach cramps from something she ate that evening, and with apologies they should leave." The double-bellied three-hundred-pound Mr. Labartine was just getting ready to tell his favorite positions with his wife when both Marbry and Jack were well out the door. By the time they got to their Volkswagen, Marbry's stomachaches had curtailed and they laughed the hour back home. Marbry took Lamaze very seriously, but Jack couldn't escape the ghost of the church-lady-turned-extraordinarily-horny Mrs. Labartine.

Jack contacted Uncle Mac, and immediately it was a relief off his shoulders to know that Mac fell right into his old story-telling mode. When Jack brought up his old friend with the priest's brother, Mac shouted, "Angus…I just saw ole Angus at Stanley Park last month." When Jack told him of his intentions, Mac comically replied, "Jack, it's too late for the priesthood…but if you're still settling to save the world, I'll call Angus right away."

"Give Uncle Mac a duty and hell, the guy always comes through," Jack said, as less than a day later he received a call from Angus MacDonald. In a brusque voice that seemed to echo another era, Angus matter-of-factly stated, "It would be my brother's pleasure to have you as his guest."

"Will he be coming out West soon?" Jack replied to the surprising invitation.

"Oh, no, I already spoke with him as soon as I got off the phone with your uncle… He wants you to be his guest at his school in Connecticut any time this spring."

"Mr. MacDonald, my wife is eight months pregnant."

"Laddy, Mr. MacDonald is my father, so call me Angus, please… Let me give you some advice…you have a dream, am I correct?"

"Yes."

"You're not getting very far with the meatheads down in Washington State, are you?"

"No."

"My brother can help you…I am going to give you his number because your wife needs you when the baby comes, and your dream needs you to act now."

"Wow," Jack thought, "this is the best directive I've gotten since Coach McC's coaching commands while playing for the Rockets! You don't second-guess yourself or your goal, you execute." Jack was on the phone with the Rev. Kenneth MacDonald of the Mt. St. John's School in Deep River, Connecticut, two minutes later.

Finishing up a treatment team meeting for juvenile offenders in Seattle, Jack picked up some salmon from Pure Food Fish Market and headed back to Bellingham. Marbry's sister Christiana was in town. The pair spent the day in Victoria and Jack would beat them home, grill some salmon, and tell Marbry about the great conversation with the "Mac Back East." Excitedly, Jack ruminated about the possibilities that meeting with him could bring.

At dinner, Christiana couldn't help herself.

"Jack, what financial gains are going to come from this? Will you be moving soon to a bigger place…after all, don't you think it's high time you did? It appears a move back East would be better for Marbry and the baby. You know, Trent says—"

Marbry cut her sister off at that point. For most of the evening, Marbry had sat still and looked awfully uncomfortable during her sister's diatribe. Jack assumed that she was at her wit's end after spending a day with her tactless sibling.

Clearing the table, Jack turned around to see Marbry's water breaking with her sister screaming as if a tsunami had hit their cozy home. Jack rushed Marbry to St. Luke's Hospital and called his mother for advice. No surprise to Jack, Marguerite and her brother Mac drove down to Bellingham, arriving by midnight. With Jack by her side, Marbry endured a tough labor through the night.

Jack felt a sense of guilt that he had disdained the Lamaze class, as everything now was real! At 6:30 a.m., a beautiful little boy came into their lives with his mother's pure vanilla skin and his father's jet-black hair. They were overjoyed.

They had briefly bounced around some family names, from Marbry's father, Walter, to her uncle, Trent, to Jack's father, Cleary, to Bennett.

"Jack, I would like to consider my father's name."

Jack had always felt that he would like his dad's name to go on in the family, but he felt that somehow he would be negating Marbry's request.

"Marbry, how about Bennett? I want our son to have the resiliency, courage, loyalty, and strength that we know is Bennett's DNA."

Marbry gazed past Jack with a look of neither agreement nor disagreement.

Bennett Walter McKenna was baptized two weeks later in Sacred Heart Church. Bennett, bristling with excitement from having Jack's firstborn named after him, used the occasion to announce his engagement to Priscilla. Billy and Marcia Bensen were named the godparents. "Bennett, since you of course always go by 'Bennett,' we will refer to little Bennett as 'Benn,' if that's all right?" Jack assured Bennett.

"I'm so honored…just so honored," Bennett answered.

Millicent and Walter did not make the christening. Their unexplained absence was quietly incomprehensible to Jack.

The invitation that Jack had to visit Father MacDonald's school would be obviously delayed, but Jack had every intention of meeting this man with the interesting residential treatment center soon enough. The little sparkling blue eyes of baby Bennett preoccupied Jack's cerebral cortex at the moment, and he simultaneously mused whether he could actually support a family trying to revolutionize an aspect of social services.

There were times when he felt a sense of admiration from Marbry for pursuing his dream, and there were other times, like the dinner with the sister, when Marbry seemed in another world, a world that begged her to escape the current one she was floating in. Often she would put a book she was reading down and stare blankly across the room.

"What are you in such contemplative thought about, Marbs?"

"I'm just reflecting on the chapter."

Jack would fight the paranoid thoughts, but frequently he felt that inside her brain something begged to escape the current world she was floating in. Now, with the birth of Benn, the abstract world melded slowly into the concrete world.

Happy Times

A year had passed and Uncle Mac's tongue-in-cheek words—"You can take a girl out of Quebec, but you can't take the Quebec out of the girl"—would often dangle in the edges of Jack's mind.

That was most apparent when summer came and the Bensens came in from Spokane; Tom came up from southern Washington; Bennett and Priscilla, living now in Santa Cruz, were in town to talk of their wedding plans; and even Arne Rosenfeld was in town with a girlfriend attending a meeting down in Seattle. Rosenfeld and a close friend of his who'd crewed with him at Princeton were invited to "a brainstorming meeting" with a Harvard dropout who was "on the cutting edge of an exciting new technology." They came up to Bellingham for the weekend along with Jack's friend Danny McDevitt from his old hockey days. Fairhaven never heard a happier, albeit rowdier, Fourth of July with that crew in town. The stories and laughter flowed endlessly that night.

Arne's friend, Gerry Francisco, was not only a Princeton legend of sorts but an Ivy League one as well. Francisco was the orchestrator of the "Mussman Muster," known all over the Ivy League. Professor Ed Mussman was not as awe-inspiring a lecturer as he was brilliant...he would often go off on tangents about his undergraduate days in "New Haven." Francisco and his cronies had the perfect antidote to liven up the class.

Francisco was able to garner a handful of ex-crew guys and a couple of track men from the Tiger team to orchestrate a "rescue mission" in the middle of class. "Borrowing" a stretcher from the McCosh Health Center, the boys were to come into the middle of Mussman's 1:00 p.m. "Public Policy" class to "rescue" the fainted Francisco. Everything was timed perfectly, as Gerry "passed out" on schedule at 1:45 p.m. The boys came in with the stretcher and, despite some awkward movements, were able to shimmy Gerry up and cart him out in a matter of minutes. The class was frozen, you could hear the proverbial pin drop, Mussman was white, and the only problem was that another student, believing it to be real, actually passed out himself. Arne laughingly told how one of the more staid students in the class, Jeff Merkley, also believing in the veracity of the staged action, attempted to take charge like a general on a battlefield… "Jeff now is working in the Office of the Secretary of Defense… Even then the guy was showing grace under pressure." The boys had to come back later to pick up the student who actually did fall. It was a good thing they did that… In a disciplinary hearing three weeks later, all charges were dismissed for "their gallantry in helping the student in need."

"What did the professor ever say to you guys?" Jack asked.

"Interestingly enough, I went into class two days later and told him thanks for bearing with us… Did you ever have that done before? He replied…'Well, we had many versions of the guerrilla theatre employed here before in the sixties and early seventies, but never that… You get an A for your creativity.' We found out months later the university wanted to burn us, but it was Mussman who convinced them to let us off after the hearing… We got to love that guy."

"Gerry, we heard a rumor that a few years ago you were responsible for a rather large endowment in Mussman's name."

"Rumors… Pass me another Rainier."

Everybody present knew it was no "rumor."

Francisco would continue those large endowments later on as a Silicon Valley corporate superstar.

Their 14th St. neighbor Davis Hughson had everybody in hysterics when he told the story of his campus job while playing football at Eastern Washington. Hughson's job was to drive the "honey buckets" from events during the off-season, returning them to the main storage center. The crew for this job was Hughson and three of his Eastern defensive line teammates. The linemen had to lift the "buckets" and make sure they were securely strapped down. After a weekend flower show, Davis and buddies were bored and tired, and "did a less than stellar job of mounting the portable toilets on the truck." Davis's supervisor, one of the nastiest football coaches on staff, started screaming, "F--- you, you son of a bitch… You're pulling away too soon." Davis, before realizing what was happening, thought the coach was shouting, "Forward, Hughson," which he had screamed all too much in routine tackling drills. Finally stopping, Hughson and the guys picked up the mess. The unfortunate thing for the coach was that the college dean and his wife, big horticulture fans in attendance, were walking out of the flower show and heard, as did everyone else in earshot, the coach's expletive deletives. The coach was called in that Monday and terminated. Hughson gleefully exclaimed, "The moral of the story is when shit flies, keep your cool."

Jack insisted Bill tell his "NoDoz" story.

"Well, if you insist... We had a econ prof...Thomas Stover... guy would put us to sleep every lecture...Mark Heth coined the perfect name for him, 'Sleepy Stover'...so one day we got every kid in class, all twenty-five of us, to come in with a box of NoDoz, and as soon as he started on his 'Stover vs. Keynes 1979 Workshop' soliloquy, we all took out our boxes, placing them prominently on our desks. After that day, Western never had a better econ prof."

Cheap Rainier beer was poured freely that night, adding to the memory and mood of the merriment. Tom took out his new acoustic-electric guitar, set up his piezoelectric pickup, and started strumming his own great tunes for everybody. The sound was a synchronicity of a blend of Culture Club, Bon Jovi, and John Cougar.

"To think we all thought Tom was just a governmental tree hugger in Oly!" Bill shouted out good-naturedly.

McDevitt, a journeyman salesman, and Jack had not seen each other in years. He covered the Northwest and heard from some former Rockets that Jack was down in the States and was able to meet up with him that July weekend. When the others turned in not long after an almost full moon shone over Bellingham Bay, the two stayed up into the wee hours of the morning talking about hockey.

"Jack, you've got to get back in the game...in some capacity... It's crazy the team from New York...the Islanders...have already won four Stanley Cup Championships!"

"It is crazy...who would think they would even have hockey there? We always grew up thinking it was just a place of gangsters and murderers," Jack added.

"Jack, that's just the point, the fans there on Long Island are diehard fans and…it's us, Canadians, who won it for them… The Long Islanders actually love those guys…Bryan Trottier, Butch Goring, Billy Harris, some other Saskatchewan guys, Billy Smith, Mike Bossy…"

"Oh, Mike Bossy…the beloved Mike Bossy…the only hockey player in the world that exists, according to Marbry."

"You gotta give it to her. He's a Montreal hometown fave. What about coaching… There's sooo much talent up in B.C. that's being untapped. Will you think about it, Jack? What people loved about you is what people loved about Butchie… remember what he said IN NEW YORK after the Islanders won their fourth?"

"Who doesn't? …'We're not the Yankees, we don't go around telling everyone how great we are. We just go out on the ice every night and show how good we are.' Every red-blooded Canadian remembers that one."

"Right on…Jacky boy, will you think about it…getting back in the game in some capacity?!"

"I will…I'm just trying to tie it all together with my juvenile reform idea."

"I'll try to see you the two or three times a year I'm in this area… We'll talk."

"Good night, Danny."

Unable to sleep that night realizing Marbry was more than a continent from her friends and family, Jack came up with an idea to have some of Marbry's old sorority sisters stay in town for a few days. Marbry was thrilled with the idea, and Agnes Rouchard and her fiancé, Tony Moritz, Liz and Will DeChamp, and Becky Latatellier all flew in on the Labor Day weekend. Jack was all set to golf, kayak, and hopefully hike with the men. Instead, the men chose a "beautiful weekend of shopping in Kirkland." Jack was intrigued by the subservience of the men. When the guests were gone, Marbry told Jack she would like to go back east with Benn in early September and stay a week or two with her family. Jack thought that would be good for her. This was as good a time as any to go back East himself. He called Father Mac, who reiterated the warm welcome to come and visit.

Jack put in for three vacation days, and after dropping off Marbry for her flight to Montreal, he would fly to New York and take the Amtrak along the beautiful Connecticut coastline, where he would be picked up at the Old Saybrook Railroad Station.

Already missing Marbry and Benn, Jack nestled in writing a plan of questions for the Rev. MacDonald. He landed at JFK Airport and the humidity reminded him of his days in Montreal. This was his first time in New York City, and the noise, commotion, and rudeness didn't diminish his expectations. It seemed a rather long taxi ride into Manhattan's Penn Station; he couldn't help but notice the amazing number of white spots along the grass on the parkway…it was litter. When the cabbie told him the fare, he realized he had been taken for a ride. He barely made his train out of Penn, and fortunately, as the train went further north, the scenery improved. Jack realized that outside of the route from JFK to Manhattan, the Northeast of the U.S. wasn't as bad as it was made out to be.

At New Haven, the train stopped for new passengers. A bespectacled man about Jack's age sat next to him. The two hit it off immediately. His name was Dan, and he had just completed a residency at Yale-New Haven Hospital, and was heading to the Old Saybrook area to complete an internship at a medical clinic.

"I'm really impressed with the scenery... I guess I've spent too much time with provincial Western Canadians to expect this," Jack admitted to Dr. Larsen.

Larsen told him, "Don't worry, I'm from the Albany, New York, area and we thought that Downstate and anywhere close to New York City would be all concrete." When Jack told him where he was headed, Larsen quickly replied, "That's the best piece of real estate in the state of Connecticut." He added, "You still seem fit... If you're planning to stick around, call me for a run." Larsen was an accomplished marathon runner who competed on a high level even through the laborious years of medical school.

Jack was picked up at the train station by one of the "prefects" from Mt. St. John's. Driving through the town of Deep River reminded Jack of the picture books his mother used to show him as a child of the New England towns with the white picket fences and the white steepled churches. They drove through two brick-columned gates dating back to 1908, and up the hill to the school along the banks of the Connecticut River. "Unbelievable, the doctor was right."

"Excuse me?" said the prefect, Rick.

"Oh, no, it's just something somebody told me about how beautiful this place was."

"The calm before the storm," quipped Rick.

Waiting on the steps of the imposing staircase was a tall, warm, burly fellow. Holding his hand out, he said in a strong New England-accented baritone voice, "Welcome, Jack. Roger Bineau. I'm the director of child care. The boys are about to line up for dinner in thirty minutes, and we'll join Father MacDonald for dinner in his dining room, but first let me show you around."

As fatigued as Jack was from his traveling, he was immediately stimulated by the structure. Bineau took him up to the third floor where the younger boys lived. The boys looked like a casting call for a Charles Dickens movie. The sound was a cacophonous melody, which immediately broke at the sight of a stranger, Jack. They were obviously well trained, as not only did the din diminish at the sight of the visitor, but they also politely introduced themselves. All of a sudden there was total silence as the supervisor called them to assemble for "lineup." He was a blond, athletic man in his mid-thirties, who seemed calm but in total control. His name was Kissinger, and Jack quipped, "You must be related to Henry, because you have better control than he does in his negotiations." There was an awkward pause, and obviously that joke had been told before, because it moved no one present.

Mr. Bineau took Jack down to the "lower dorms," where the older boys, or "residents" as they were referred to, lived. They went past the gym and briefly headed to the outside fields, and Bineau made it a point to show Jack a mowed-out grass trail circling a beautiful view of the river and what turned out to be Gillette's Castle across it in the distance. Apparently, a prefect, which Jack figured out to be what they named the boy's counselors, by the name of Tommy Green had constructed a cross-country course.

"We just had a cross-country race here," Bineau said proudly, "against one of the local prep schools…it was a beautiful thing… our inner-city boys who have nothing got in shape to beat those boys who have everything! Tommy even got some of the kids who smoke to train for this."

This was music to Jack's ears. Feeling like a gung-ho kid, Jack said to Mr. Bineau, "Why can't the residential centers in the state of Washington have this structure and the outlets for physical activity that I see you have here?"

"You like it, Jack? Good, make sure you tell Father MacDonald what you just told me."

As they approached Father MacDonald's dining room off the main lobby, there was an air of formality within the room. Waterford glasses and Lenox china were in stark contrast to the 1950s diner plates and glasses in the "residents' dining hall." When Father walked in, Jack had to hide his amusement within of his memory of the man visiting Angus MacDonald he and his friends had thought was Santa Clause when Jack was a child. He had a cherubic yet aged and dignified presence. His Scotsman's air of confidence was a carbon copy of Uncle Mac's. He possessed a combination of the presence of a pontiff and a smile that told otherwise. Mr. Bineau, Father, Jack, and a man named Tom, who had an imposing presence but was barely introduced, other than "Tom has been here ten years," sat down for dinner.

Father referred to Jack as Mr. McKenna, and it reaffirmed his dominating presence in the room. Jack had a retinue of questions prepared for Father MacDonald, but he did not think this the time and place to ask them. Father insisted on hearing about Uncle Mac back home. If only Mac knew the reverence this Catholic priest had for him, he might minimize his anti-Catholicism, Jack mused.

"Your uncle was quite a hero…known all across the provinces for his gallantry in World War II, and I only knew of your father, but not only we Canadians, but the world really, Mr. McKenna, benefitted from the South Saskatchewan brigade and all those who fought at Dieppe. You know, Mr. McKenna, while the raid itself was not totally successful, the Allies learned a lot, and it was the reason for the Allied success at the Normandy beach heads at D-Day."

Jack knew there was a reason he had to come here to meet this man. He now felt that if nothing else was gained from his trip, coming close to three thousand miles and hearing somebody giving the respect members of his family and his brave countrymen deserved made it all worthwhile.

"Monumentally worthwhile," he would later tell Bennett and Billy Bensen. "Too many Canadians have forgotten our most courageous countryman for too long. You are never too old to be told of the great things your family was part of."

After dinner it was just Father MacDonald and Jack speaking about Canadian history, juvenile reform, religion, and even a little hockey. The greatest insight he received from the reverend that night was to "Be patient with the bureaucrats…never let them out-frustrate you." Jack knew those words were from a credible source, as although Mt. St. John's was run by the Diocese of Norwich, a Catholic Church affiliate, they received some substantial funding from both the state and federal government. Father had to balance running and keeping the structure he had in place going while placating the village of Deep River, the state and its multitudinal agencies, and the federal government. Father himself was quite a conservative-sounding Catholic, but a socially muscular liberal.

Jack would be staying down in one of the prefect's residences, two brick homes adjacent to the entrance of the property. Father offered to drive him down the hill there. Jack opted to walk, as it had been a long, heady, but fulfilling day, and he wanted to stroll down the beautiful country road and digest everything he took in on the day. He was longing to speak to Marbry. The house he was staying at, very much a male domicile, was a tad noisy and limited on privacy. They had a wall phone outside the kitchen. He gathered enough quarters and made the long-distance call to Montreal. Jack wanted to convey to the love of his life how almost surreal the day had been for him, but ended up having a surreal call with Marbry.

Marbry would be staying in what Millicent, Marbry's mother, referred to as the "Pearl Guest Room." It was white from ceiling to floor with pearl-shell paintings and pearl decorum that Jack referred to as "on steroids." The room faced west, and was without a view. Views were very important to Millicent; everywhere "Well" and she went in their myriad travels, a room with a view was insisted upon. In lieu of a view, Millicent's intention was to make her guests feel "both rich and at the seashore." If you wanted to get close to Millicent, as if that were an easy task, a good way might be to ask her about the "views" she had seen. Don't dare ask her about her political views.

Grant, the butler, answered the phone.

"Of course, I'll get Ms. Marbry."

"Hmmm," Jack thought, "okay, Ms. Marbry?!"

The sound of Marbry's voice soothed Jack's longing for her. "Jack, oh, Jack, how are you, darling, how charming to hear from you. I just put Benn to bed."

"Mar…I really miss you both…I have so much to tell you… things have gone really well."

"Does that mean you will be making more money, Jack?"

At that moment one of the prefects who lived at the house Jack was staying in came in the room, in earshot of Jack, just in time for Jack to purposely disconnect the phone.

Gathering himself, he called Marbry back.

"Jack, we must have been disconnected."

"Yes, poor connection, it must be the thunderstorms we are getting here...I was telling you about how fruitful my day was and..."

"Jack, guess who's here visiting us at Mother's and Wellington's?"

"Let me guess...Mike Bossy?"

"Now wouldn't that be charming?! No, much better, Jack, Uncle Trent...and I have bigger news! Christiana is here with her fiancé."

"Whaaat...didn't we see your sister two months ago or so... and wasn't she single?"

"Yes, Jack, but Monroe is such a darling...Trent matched up the two...it's so romantic."

"Let me guess...he's selling investments...?"

"Oh, no, Jack he's a very successful car salesman like Trent was...he drives the most adorable red Porsche. Jack, you must be so tired, I know I am."

"Yeah, Marbry, maybe we get our rest and I'll call tomorrow!"

"Charming, Jack, charming...love you." Two words Jack had never heard Marbry utter ever before—"charming" and "darling"; he'd heard them six times in less than four minutes from her. As tired as he was, Jack didn't sleep a wink that night.

The next day, Jack sprang up because he wanted to take everything in before his early evening flight out of Hartford's Branford Airport. Jack ate breakfast with the resident boys, and again, he was most impressed with their orderly behavior.

At midday he attended a "staff meeting." It was a weekly meeting held every Wednesday in the conference room with Mr. Bineau at the head of a long table and the prefects at the sides. The prefects all were athletic-looking young men ranging from right out of college to late thirties. Sports was their mantra. The buzz in the room was the state of basketball in the Big East Conference. The discussions were lively and feisty, but at 9:30 a.m., as scheduled, the meeting came to order. Roger Bineau started it with a prayer for UCONN's basketball team. This was the second year, "seemingly since the beginning of time," as one prefect named Gil said, "that the Huskies are tapping on the top-twenty door." Most of the young men were graduates of Catholic liberal arts schools from the Northeast, and one was an ex-seminarian.

Prior to the meeting, a couple of the guys had Gary, the former seminarian, tell Jack the story he was apparently most known for. Two years earlier, he'd taken ten boys who had earned "privilege points" during the week to a Pawtucket Red Sox game against the Rochester Red Wings. Pawtucket was less than an hour away from Deep River and excitement abounded. The game was tied at one each at the end of the ninth inning. Gary called Mr. Bineau, letting him know the game was going into extra innings. Roger, in a pre-Easter-holiday good mood, told him, "Gary, stay to the end of the game." Good thing Gary did not stay to the end of the game. The game was called at 4:07 a.m. and it remains the longest professional baseball game ever played. Meanwhile, Roger, by 1:30 a.m. fearing the worst, called the Connecticut State Troopers. Fortunately, Gary had decided somewhere between the twenty-first and the twenty-second inning it was time to go. Most of the boys had been used to being escorted home alongside the stark blue State Trooper cars, but for Gary it was a first.

Jack observed two things that seemed radiant to him. These "prefects" were a darn good bunch of regular guys who had healthy interests, and they cared about the kids they supervised. The structure was the structure! He knew he could bring this model out West with him. That night he went out with several of the prefects down at the favorite watering hole, Russ's...nickel beers and hot dogs he cooked right in front of you...Jack's visit couldn't be more complete.

When he got back to the house, he called Marbry, again bristling with excitement and forgetting about the previous night's call.

"Marbry, another great day...how was yours?"

"Jack, I wish you were here. I had such exciting conversations with Uncle Trent about investments we should make."

"Marbry, wait a minute...what the fuck?!"

As soon as it came out, Jack wished it hadn't.

"Jack, what's happening to you? I've never heard you use an obscenity to anyone! I'm hurt...have you changed...what's gotten into you, darling?"

"I'm sorry, Marbry, I wish I could explain what's gotten into me."

When Jack thanked Mr. Bineau for his hospitality, Roger announced in a fain assist, "Make sure you stop by Father MacDonald on ya way out." His New England orotund twang augmenting the warmth of the man. MacDonald came down from the perch of the second-floor stairs, holding on gingerly to the bannisters that beckoned a palisade-like fortress to the resident boys, if they dared attempt to enter that "off-limits" area. They all knew and respected that the area was "off-limits," but not the man.

"Leaving us a little later than expected, Mr. McKenna…I hope you found everything in order and helpful for your own career objectives."

"Yes, Father, I confess I got so taken in that I had to call Branford Airport and try to get on another flight, but the only flight out would be tonight down at JFK. So one of the off-duty prefects, Tommy Green, is going to drive me to the train station."

"Oh, yes, Mr. Green, good generous young man…he's from the golden ghetto, you know."

"Golden ghetto, where's that?"

"Ask him, I kid him all the time about it—that's my term for Long Island… He takes it in good stride, partly because we think he's become a converted Connecticut Yankee, ha ha."

Jack enjoyed the humor in what seemed to be an inside joke for this jovial man of the cloth.

"One last thing, Mr. McKenna, make sure you tell your uncle Mac hello—he's one of the greats! I'm praying for him. I'm no less of a skeptic than he, and you know even WE can be saved."

The comment took Jack off guard. It disabused any prior notion Jack had that Father MacDonald was unaware of Mac's visceral Catholic bigotry.

"Will do, and thank you so much for everything," Jack commented, trying to block his mind of the imaginary nimbus he thought he saw around Father MacDonald.

Tommy Green took Jack to the Old Saybrook railroad station. Green seemed to be an adventurous sort—as he inquired to Jack,

"You have a little time now for the six o'clock Amtrak train…you mind if I drive you the scenic way back along River Road?"

Jack readily complied, as that was malmsey to his voice. Green pointed out the scenery and landmarks, and he now knew what Father MacDonald meant in describing Green as a possible "converted Connecticut Yankee."

Taking a shot, Jack smiled and said, "Heard you hail from the golden ghetto?"

"Oh, I see you were talking with Father Mac."

"Yes…I'm not so sure I get the golden ghetto joke."

"Oh, yeah, Father Mac's a kidder. But there're a lot of people up here, out West, I'm sure where you are, that think where I'm from we all are these bombastic people living in the lap of luxury, just showing off our wealth, greedy as all get out…there're more than a few of those folk down there, but…"

Immediately cutting Tommy off, Jack chimed in, "Trust me, they're everywhere."

The train ride through most of Connecticut was magnificent, and Jack dozed off musing about all that he had taken in. Other than the fuliginous frame of the factory-appearing city of Bridgeport, Jack found a breathtaking beauty in what he saw. He could hardly wait to share his whole experience with all back home.

Approaching Vancouver International, the plane juddered about before landing, an air turbulence he hadn't experienced.

Rocking More Than the Obvious

JACK FLEW INTO VANCOUVER INTERNATIONAL and waited for Marbry and Benn's flight to land a few hours later. Sitting off the baggage-claim area, Jack heard an old familiar voice chirping its way to him.

"Jack, Jack?"

He got up, nearly falling over his luggage.

"Rosemary, how are you?"

Spoken in a voice that was one quarter stevedore, one quarter professor, and one half sex goddess, the words came from Rosemary Ryan, known affectionately as "Rosemary the Rocker." Rosemary was a flash from Jack's past, long before he left hockey and long before he went back East to McGill. "What are you doing, Jack...you look lonely, you puppy dog, you."

"I'm waiting for my wife," he answered as Rosemary she moved her shadowy eyes on Jack's bags.

"Oh, yes, I heard you got married..."

Jack asked the question he already knew the answer to... "What about you, Rosemary, you married?"

"Jack, still nobody good enough for me... You know all those hockey gamers are down in the States or are married... I'm still very much free. Jack, I have to rush...but I'm still up in Pemberton...and if you check around...I still keep my old friends close."

Whatever Rosemary the Rocker meant by that was foreign to Jack. The nickname given to Rosemary had nothing to do with her affinity for rock 'n' roll. Scotty Cournoyer found that out when he, in good faith, wanting to impress her with a concert opportunity, had secured tickets for the Bachman-Turner Overdrive concert at Empire Stadium. Scott prepared himself for a great night for "Taking Care of Business" with a freshly bought bag of quality Fraser Valley weed. Not even able to take one toke and initially disappointed at Rosemary's haste to leave the concert, Scotty discovered "rocking out to sounds" wasn't her gig. Rosemary had her own rocking in mind. No complaints came from Scotty later that night for missing most of the sold-out concert.

Hockey guys, always fit-looking, always carrying the aura of strength and health, most of them handsome of complexion and features, were given undue exaggerated rumors for their "sexploits." True hockey guys never had time for extra "extracurricular activities," the way their counterparts in professional basketball and football to the south seemed to enjoy. Nevertheless they loved the "rep" they always received.

A gentle kiss and a dismissive hug was not what Jack longed for, but it was what he received from his longed-for Marbry. Benn seemed to squeeze out more affection to his dad; the smile and wide-open eyes were what every father lived for from his child. That smile reignited an indelible image that often flashed across the interiors of his cerebral cortex. It was a card from his father for his mother, Marguerite. The hand-written note simply read, "Thank you for our love. Thank you for our boys. You are everything to me, you are my lager of life." Jack understood his father not to be defined by his romantic ways, but he sensed his incredible love for this incredible woman.

Marguerite kept it on her desk, centered on top of a white-laced cover along with the pictures of the four of them, like they were relics from a sacred past too fleeting, too distant, to actually be real. Jack was too young to remember his father, but that card always spoke to him of the depth of his dad's love for his mother, Preston, and him.

Jack carried Benn into the house. It was easy to notice the firmness with which Marbry placed her luggage down in the front hall, foreshadowing a trove of thoughts about to be released aloud. Jack seemed to be the one conscious of putting Benn to bed, and when he did, Marbry, gesticulating about the foyer, greeted him with a folder of papers.

"Jack, could you at least look at these...?"

"Sure, Marbs, well, how was your trip?"

"Jack, this was my trip...just loook at these, please!" With letterhead that read "Reynolds, Carey, and Doertz," neatly placed inside was a stock portfolio with significant investments that had Marbry's signature on the bottom. Puzzled by the content of the portfolio and the intensity of Marbry's mood, he tried with great effort to maintain an open tone in his voice.

"So I see you made some investments with Trent, using, I'm presuming, a little bit of our savings."

"Precisely, my love. I went ahead and did it for us, you, little Benn, and me. Before you say anything, Jack, I balance the checkbook, I manage our finances; oddly enough, you never initiate any financial conversation."

Raising his voice, Jack retorted, "Marbs, we do fine. Since I'm on the road often, I trust what you are doing with our savings… What do we need to talk about? I found the house, I got the mortgage, everything I get, I give to you…why do we need all of a sudden a very formal conversation…and it looks like the person who wants a financial conversation went ahead and invested before a conversation was had!"

"Don't raise your voice at me! I'm doing what YOU should have done a long time ago! What is our future without finances?!"

Jack breathed hard. He amazed himself that he was able to take a conciliatory stance among the ugliest mood he'd ever seen Marbry display.

His gut churning, he mustered, "We should probably sit down, Marbry," he said. "These look good, where do I have to sign?"

"Jack, it's done."

The whole time away from Marbry he'd thought about getting home and making love all night with her. There was no lovemaking that night. There wasn't even a kiss.

"Silly that I pitied the desperate Rosemary the Rocker earlier," Jack thought as Marbry fell fast asleep.

Searching

"JACK, DO YOU EVER MISS hockey?" Bennett asked Jack over several bottles of ale at the Out and Out Tavern.

"Honestly, at first it was like this huge reprieve, then I started to miss it every day…but so much now going on, I've gotten over it…I do feel it's ironic that my family eventually got on with the idea that I was out of the game better than I did after a while."

"I've got be honest with you, Jack, I feel you gave up a lot… the noises of the crowd, the brotherhood of your teammates, not to mention you could have made a pretty good living…and you would have."

"Bennett, what are you talking about? You were one of our nation's top runners, or was I reading the wrong press or what… you could have healed, but you left that for something else, something new!"

"It's different in my sport, Jack. You have to be one of the best in the world to get a lucrative shoe contract…the Kenyans and the Ethiopians are running in the low 3:30s for 1500…a lot of them. Besides, there is that element that to get that far, some feel you've got to sell out your body!"

"What…drugs?"

"Yeah, you remember the guy who beat me out at my last NCAAs, when Jumbo moved me up to the 5000...Jay Slope of Oregon?"

"I do remember that kick...didn't he run 13:18?"

"Yes, and he hung up his spikes soon after competing in Europe for a year and started an athletic apparel company that is really taking off. He's operating out of Eugene, Oregon, and he is on the pulse of everything in the sport. He told me that you are in the 'one percent if you're clean'...people always talk about the altitude-trained Kenyans...Jay insists that they are getting what he calls 'help.' It's insane...I don't want to take anything that diminishes my pecker."

Bennett went on, his tone waxing sentimentally. "Switching to triathlon was like finding something new and genuine, like finding Priscilla. There's a code of honor in Triathlon. Geez, Jack, they manufacture bikes in this sport just to prevent 'drafting!' There truly is this sense of respect for your body, your training, and your competitors like you used to describe about hockey...a brotherhood of tough gamers...remember you told me that?"

"I do...and I also remember how shocked we all were when you could swim...let alone two and a half miles!"

"Jack, the most important thing to me in life is Priscilla, and living up to the honor that you gave to me with little Benn."

"Don't forget his baptismal name is Bennett Walter," Jack chimed, "sort of balances out the honor quotient."

Bennett laughed. "We want to take a stab at this, then settle down and have a Fresin for Benn."

"Fresin? What the freak is a Fresin?"

"A friend cousin. Right now we want to embrace the challenge...but I don't want to end up like Gracchus and have a ship with no rudder, driven by the wind that blows in the undermost region of death."

"Bennett, you quoting Tolstoy?"

"Kafka, Jack, Kafka…I did more than run at Villanova, you know!"

"It is sort of Kafkaesque that here you are, Bennett, the noble, competitive athlete, and me the rogue searching, still searching."

"You know, Jack, you have to spend so much time on the bike, sometimes when I'm on my Cervelo, I feel like maybe I am absolutely nuts for chasing this dream…"

"Bennett, chase it for the both of us."

"Jack, you probably don't remember this, but when you were playing in the Juniors and getting all that attention, I'll never forget that quote you had posted in your basement about Terry O'Reilly. I was surprised, because it was a quote about a Boston Bruin by the Boston coach, and you weren't a Bruins fan… remember what you said to me when I questioned you about it?"

"I do remember what I said," Jack said coyly.

Bennett went on. "Yeah, you said, 'it's not the team that guy plays for, it's what he's saying, DUMMY'…and I still remember to this day you calling me that, and what the quote you had hanging up said."

"Refresh my memory…what did it say?"

"The coach said, 'No one works harder. No one runs down the other team so much or lifts his team so much. He's quite a guy, who doesn't know when to quit.'"

"Pretty good memory for a dummy," Jack said, bringing Bennett to a howl.

"Jack, that's the guy I always want to be…and you and Mac, even Preston when we were young, taught me that. Jack, you know what's most important, and I don't feel crazy saying this, but we are both romantics AND fighters, and we'll always be that to the end."

"To the end," Jack cheered as together they hoisted a cold Labatt.

Bloom off the Rose

RADIANT RED CROCOSMIA, FULLY WRAPPING the backyard of Jack and Marbry's house, always brought some expected visitors winging and whirling their way around the yard. The hummingbirds, suckled in by the nectar of this genus "Lucifer," were a favorite of little Benn. He giggled profusely at the marvel of those winged creatures. This weekend afternoon Jack had Benn and the garden ambience all to himself. Marbry went into town with her newfound friends from the book club she had joined for an "afternoon tea and shopping spree." Benn's wonder at the hummingbirds' buzzing voices never tired and Jack's contentment at Benn's laughter reverberating around the yard never got old. Jack took Benn's little pudgy legs and tickled them for added delight until he fell fast asleep. Jack put him in the downstairs room off the front hall they kept for Benn with its west-side bay windows draped in sunlight. Adjacent to that was a little closet of a room, really a mudroom, which they kept as their "office." The phone rang, and Jack was able to pick it up with Benn still sleeping. It was Marguerite, Jack's mom.

"Jack, if you two aren't going to come up to B.C. with my grandson, I'm coming down there."

"Mom…that would be great… Let me just check with Marbs when she gets back. We'll work out what's good."

"Jack, I would like to come down any week in July or August and get together with Tom as well; maybe you could invite him up to your place."

As he was speaking to Marguerite, Jack couldn't help but notice a strange checkbook off to the right on the desk sticking out under some mail. It more than startled him. "Mom…I'll call you back tonight."

"Everything all right, dear?"

"Yes, I'll get back to you."

The checkbook was under "Marbry McKenna" and it was a separate account he had never seen. There was a small pink ledger underneath, and what caught Jack's eye was the amount of money made out to local grocery stores. Hundreds and hundreds of dollars over a two-week period. "Hmm, could Marbry be a secret hoarder of food?" Actually, the refrigerator was sparse, and food shopping looked like it should be more of a priority if anything.

When Marbry came back, figuring he could prompt some grocery talk, he asked her if she should go grocery shopping. "That's all right, Jack. We are eating out tonight. I'll take care of it Monday when you are at work."

Checks, money, a lot of money. Groceries. He couldn't figure out why, but he couldn't stop thinking about it. Tuesday when he had a little more time as he was on the way down to a treatment team meeting in Seattle, Jack stopped in a local Albertsons. Meticulously, Jack began to price out what a week's grocery bill might be. The fifty-three-dollar total he priced out was far short of the six hundred dollars of checks made to the store.

Coming home that night, he went into the home office and, checking around, he couldn't locate either the strange new checkbook or their joint account.

"Marbs, where is our checkbook?"

"Jack, why are you asking for that? I balance all the checking for us."

"Well, Marbry, I thought about what you said, and you are right, I need to be involved more with our finances."

"Okay, Jack, let's look at it tomorrow."

"Marbry, I'd like to look at it now."

"It's not important, Jack."

"To me it is!" Jack retorted, now angrily.

Going into the kitchen, Marbry went for her pocketbook, dug in, and grabbed a checkbook, throwing it at Jack, missing his eye with the venomous velocity she threw it.

Jack threw it back at her, saying, "Just keep it, if it means that much to you."

Finances were not discussed for another month. It was also not the time to have his mother down for a visit, so Jack waited to ask another time, another day.

The next morning Marbry, in a sober tone, told Jack some news. "Jack…I'm going to work."

"Marbry…wow, that's great, where?"

"The Lowenthals' Nursery and Gallery…Chelsea, a gal in my book club, is a waitress at the Bayou, and she knows everybody in town… She put me in touch with the Lowenthal family… They have that nursery and gallery north of town."

"I know it well, Marbs… I bought our first rhododendrons there that I planted in the east garden for you, not to mention all those roses… The guy, the owner, Art, is a sweetheart. I hit it off with him immediately…amazingly enough he recognized my name… He told me besides his family he had two loves… horticulture and hockey."

Arthur Lowenthal and his family were one of the best-known and best-loved family-run businesses in the northwest corridor of the Northwest. Art was the third generation of a successful business that sold flowers and native sculpture and artifacts from the great Northwest. Not only did folks here love them for their warmth, honesty, and affability, but the family also donated two hundred acres adjacent to their property to the county, a preserve open to the public with trails winding through beaver ponds, mature old-growth forests, and placid wetlands.

"Yes…they are lovely, and they love the fact that I speak another language for the tourist customers that come over the border. Jack, I start the week after next, but this week I'm going back East."

"Whaaat?! Marbry, Marguerite…she wants naturally to spend some time with Benn and us…and is looking to come down, well, soon."

"Your mother will wait, Jack. We have important things going on… My family is having a sendoff party for Trent, as he is moving his company to New York."

"New York?"

"Yes, Trent is really gaining some prestige as an investor. That's why I'm sooo glad you agreed with me to have him handle our investments…"

"Did I have a choice?" Jack mumbled under his breath.

"I know you probably can't get off work with short notice… so…"

To her surprise, Jack cut her off. "Marbry, I'll take a week of the three I get… I'm going to be with you."

"If you can enjoy my family, and honor Trent, good," Marbry shot back.

Without even knowing it, Jack was slowly being caught in the fog of placating every whim and desire of Marbry. He rationalized it in his own mind by believing that, going back to Montreal, there would be a rekindling of romantic walks through Cap Saint-Jacques, or a simple picnic at Parc La Fontaine. If he had to put up with another celebration of the family deity Trent, so be it.

The romantic time ended up being as fleeting as the long weekend itself. What was special was spending time with Benn and Marbry, and Helene, Trent's ex, and her children. Marbry seemed at her most relaxed with Helene, and from all accounts it was impressive that she even invited the family. Millicent and Walter did not even acknowledge their presence at the party or elsewhere. Millicent was busy walking around controlling everything…or trying to assume that position, whatever the necessity of it. Walter looked more like the undertaker at a wake… he seemed unusually subdued. Witnessing their dismissiveness of Helene and children, Jack understood the meaning of "the family outlaws" well.

Helene's was a beautiful family, the children well-behaved and cheery, and yet they were as welcomed with the Wellingtons as coal brownies at a Sierra Club gathering. The children pushed Benn on the park swings as he cooed for more. Jack played street hockey with the boys, and the youngest girl, Rae-Ann, kept asking him for "piggy-back rides." The reignited romance with Marbry did not materialize over the weekend, but Jack's love for children and family was palpable to everyone. Not felt mutually by others, but palpably recognized.

Flying back west, Jack asked the dreaded question, "Marbry, how could your family treat Helene and her kids so coldly?"

Looking out the airplane window as it flew over the Canadian Rockies, Marbry just answered, "Families are complex, Jack. You should know full well."

They didn't speak much on the flight, but the one conversation that went well was that it was decided mutually that Jack would write all checks, pay all bills, and be communicated with on all "investments."

When they arrived home, there was an important-sounding message left on the answering machine from Ron Legion, Jack's immediate boss, asking Jack to call him as soon as possible when he got in.

"Jack, can you come down to Tacoma in the morning? We have a proposal for you."

At nine o'clock in the morning Jack learned, among other things, the dearth of geographical knowledge many adults have.

"Jack, I want you to meet Sam Wenthoff. He is on our board of directors and he is very impressed with your latest field report and résumé."

Mr. Wenthoff fit the mold to a tee of the "bespectacled bureaucrats hovering around just south of Burien," as Tom had described to Jack one night.

"Mr. McKenna, our board is interfacing with agencies outside of Washington, and with your experience and vision, we would like you to run one of our group homes for homeless children and P.I.N. S. in Vancouver. I understand that's where you're originally from?"

Immediately, Jack thought, "Okay, I'm back home in Canada, and the commute won't be so bad."

"Yes, I understand my native country's government really wants to combine their resources with ours with this critical work," Jack offered. Jack's boss and Mr. Wenthoff looked puzzled.

Mr. Wenthoff went on to say, "Jack, we do understand it's a big move for you, but the sale of your house would be a net gain, and you and your family of course would live rent-free in the home itself."

"Move?" The reality of the disconnection in communication set in like a blade to his throat. "We are talking Vancouver, B.C., correct, gentleman?"

The two men laughed ruefully, "Jack, Vancouver, Washington—as some of our friends in state government call it, the north suburb of Portland, Oregon."

Jack froze.

Mr. Wenthoff was saying something officious-sounding, but it was a mere murmur to Jack. Realizing Jack's disconnection, Legion chimed in, "Jack, sounds good, it's everything you wanted to move along with."

"Yeees, gentleman, thank you for the offer, when do I get back to you?"

Legion, now looking ruffled, said, "Jack...since when is the state a corporation? This is a directive to go into effect the first of the year."

Wenthoff got up, saying he was just going to get some water.

With Jack and Ron alone, the tension tore through the conference room.

"Jack, you are kidding, aren't you? This is what you wrote about...this is why we hired you, so when something like this came along...this is YOU...there is no turning back...this is what the state, Wenthoff, I...this is what you are going to do!"

Words Worth Their Weight

"THIS IS WHAT YOU ARE going to do!" The words hit Jack hard.

The tonality of the words. The finality of the words. His head hadn't bothered him so much since he got slashed and fell head first into the boards in one of his last games with the Rockets. He couldn't wait to tell Bennett those words, that choice—or, more aptly, that lack of choice.

Bennett and Priscilla were training in Albuquerque for seven weeks and were hard to reach. The phone rang and it was Tom, his cousin.

"I hear how you uninvited your mom to your place!"

"Well, it's a little more involved than that... You have time to talk?"

"It sounds urgent... What's up?"

"Maybe you can pull a few governmental strings, Tom. I have been given an ultimatum." Tom listened as Jack told him the proposal he was given.

"Wow...well, I guess things are pretty blue in the red, white, and blue for you, Jack," Tom said in a poor attempt bringing humor to the situation.

"Worse than that, things are not that great with Marbry, and asking her to a) move and b) share a home for homeless children would be like asking Queen Elizabeth to move to East London, and I'm talking London, Ontario."

"Oh, so reality has hit?!"

"What is that supposed to mean?"

"Jack, listen, we need to talk…and the reason I'm calling is I'm going up to Vancouver, B.C…yes, British Columbia, not Washington, this weekend…and I rented a nice little place in Horseshoe Bay with this fabulous woman I met down here who turns out to be from Alberta… We have a lot of room, and I thought it would be good for you and Marbry and the baby to come up…not to mention YOU need to see your mom."

"How did you guys meet?" Jack queried.

"Where else…at an environmental rally at Evergreen State."

"Of course."

"We actually just started talking about music and she asked me to come to a Heavens to Betsy jam at one of the clubs in Olympia."

"She asked you…Heavens to what?"

"Yeah, Jack…it's one of the top Riot grrrl groups."

"Riot what?"

"Jack…it's alternative rock…you know, indie…their lyrics are important stuff—political, environmental, feminist concerns. The sound is bold. Hey…when you were hitting hockey pucks all day in Vancouver, there was a group up there called Mecca Normal—they freaking started it all… Now down here in Olympia and Seattle there is just this whole huge DIY thing going on in music… It's powerful."

"DIY, Tom, I thought only the military speaks in acronyms!"

"Do It Yourself! Jack…you'll dig Rachel…she's cool…strong…independent…beautiful…and she knows music."

"Tom…I'm there, and I'm bringing up Benn. Marbry is working the weekend…"

"Wait, Marbry is working? You ought to take back the queen quote."

"Funny, but all too true, Tom!"

"Cool, Rachel will dig the fact that your lady is getting her own space and time...cool."

Any time Jack went back home he always appreciated the warmth his mother had created in the home. The domestic cherry hardwood floors glowed sharply as if Marguerite had polished them an hour before. They'd looked this way three decades ago and mirrored the foundation that Marguerite had built as a long-time working single parent with two boys. The immaculate, spotless rugs, drapes, and curtains were something that only a boy who comes home after a long time appreciates. The pictures of him as a baby with his mom, dad, and Preston sparkled as if they were taken last week.

Tom and Rachel Beliveau drove Jack and Benn up to B.C. They stopped in for a visit with Marguerite, who was ecstatic to see them all. As Jack completed his least favorite activity, changing Benn's diaper, Marguerite took Tom and Rachel in the kitchen. She had just baked a fresh loaf of her famous zucchini bread, from the zucchinis grown in her garden. The garden was a metaphor for Marguerite's existence. It was a spectacular garden in an unspectacular yard space she took care of so well, nurturing it the way she did Jack and his brother. She insisted they stay for dinner, but Tom knew Jack had much to speak with his mom about, and Jack didn't want to prevent Tom from spending any time with Rachel, a most handsome woman with a soft, gentle voice.

It was good for Jack to spend some time with his mother. Watching her hug and play with little Benn brought back forgotten memories of the loving giant he was blessed to be born to. She always seemed steady, grounded, unmoved by the vagaries of life. While he felt affection from her, she never allowed emotion or sadness to ease out of her uneasy life. Jack often felt that this was a trait lost on him. Her matter-of-fact outlook on life, the sheer honesty of it, was sometimes too much to bear for a son with an innate streak of idealism. Preston was more like his mother, his sharp honesty easily sometimes to be mistaken for cynicism. Perhaps this was why Jack avoided her over the years, something that Marguerite seemed to understand and not use as a "mother's crutch" when he did come home. Jack had met a lot of strong and noble people in his life, but he was well into his thirties when he realized his mother had something few others had. Marguerite Sawchuck McKenna was a creature of love; a judger of others she was not.

Their conversation was the best and indeed the most necessary they ever had as mother and son. She listened as Jack lamented how he was worried about his wife.

"Marbry seems so affected by her family back home, specifically her uncle, not to mention some of her friends in Bellingham."

"You're getting like the Americans, so afraid of others," Marguerite replied.

"I never knew you to feel that way, Mom."

"Jack, we all are affected by who we are, where we are, and what the societal expectations are...that's the thing your uncle Mac was most concerned about with you living down in the States...a lot of contrived pressures, it seems, down there. By the way, before you go back...please stop and see your uncle...his health hasn't been well of late."

Truth Delayed

UNCLE MAC INSISTED ON MEETING the three for Sunday brunch at the very popular breakfast spot Roundel's in downtown Vancouver. Knowing Tom's affection for Mac, Jack called him to join them. Tom had only one sure-fire response, "We're there."

Looking thinner but more robust than Marguerite had made him out, Mac was his vintage old-school self. When Tom and Rachel walked in, Mac took her hand, kissing it, and explained, "They have it all here. The vegetarian dishes are supposed to be sumptuous as well."

Rachel turned to Tom, happily saying, "That was so nice of you to tell him I was a vegetarian." Tom never had. Mac just seemed to have that gift of reading people, even their palate choices.

"So, Jack, how's saving the world?"

"Still can't get a new line, Uncle Mac? You and Marbry seem to share in the list of most unoriginal lines."

"Well, Angus told me they loved you in Connecticut, and if you were going to stay in the States, you can't go wrong with that reverend and the operation he runs…plus you can always trust a Canadian at heart!"

"Well, since you asked, and we are all here together…I'm leaving social services."

Silence reigned for a long second at the table.

Even Rachel, unknown to Jack until two days before, looked surprised.

"How does Marbry feel about that, Jack?" Marguerite asked.

"Marbry, if you must know, is at war with the fact that I'm an idealist living, to quote her, 'in a Don Quixote world.'"

"I'm impressed she's familiar with the character," Tom quipped, getting a healthy elbow in the side from his soft- and gentle-spoken lady friend.

"When did you come to this decision?" Marguerite again inquired.

"Last night...I mean yesterday...I mean now."

Turning to Mac and Marguerite, Jack said, "Tom and you and Bennett are the closest family I have, so it just makes sense to let your family know all the important stuff. The good news is that the position I was told I must take doesn't start until the first of next year, so I figure I have two months to keep working, give them the proper notice they deserve, and figure everything out."

"Well, to figuring everything out," Tom bellowed out as the Bloody Marys arrived.

When Mac got up, Jack had to ask Mac the question that had been bothering him for years.

"Uncle Mac...I need to ask you this. Remember that steelhead-fishing trip in Northern B.C. when I was seven, when we 'needed to sip in the Skeena River'?"

"Of course, Jack."

"Why DID you leave us alone for so long in the middle of nowhere...whose test of manhood was that...yours or Mr. Johnstone's?"

"Jack, test of manhood...BULLSHIT...you never figured that out...I figured you were smarter than that...we were lost."

Tom looked over at Mac. He now noticed the unhealthy pallor Marguerite was referring to that Mac had had recently.

Embarrassment

"JACK, WHAT'S THIS STORY YOUR mom told us about you and a guitar?" Tom queried as they pulled out on a balmy night, heading south out of Vancouver back to the States.

"Yeah...well, Tom, you inspired me a little. You know I never had any musical-instrument lessons growing up, so when I heard you playing again, I figured I'd get a guitar, I'd get a self-lesson book, and maybe you could help me learn when I saw you...so I ordered a Fender American Standard Stratocaster."

"Jack, cool...that's a very good guitar. So what happened, Jack? Is it true it was returned?"

"Well, yeah."

"You returned it?"

"No, Marbry did," said Jack, lowering his voicing, looking out the window.

Rachel let out a mild obscenity, seemingly raucous for such a collected woman.

"Why?"

"Well, it came in a big box, and I was waiting for the weekend to open it up and use it...but Marbs felt it was just taking up space and that I'd 'be too busy to use it'...I don't know...I guess she was right...I don't know."

There was a deafening silence for several minutes until Rachel, turning to Jack, cast her deep exotic eyes on him. "Jack,

I have something you can say sweetly to Marbry. When I was at university, in one of my music history and theory classes we studied an American nineteenth-century poet and musician, Sidney Lanier. One of the great things he said was 'Music is love in search of words'...tell her that, Jack."

"Thanks, RB, I'll wait for the right moment."

Jack knew that Rachel was in fact telling him to ask Marbry for the instrument back. What she didn't know was that Jack was on a quest not just for music, not just for words, but for the love that was oozing out of him for Marbry to come oozing back again out of her.

Crossing back into Washington, Jack asked, "Tom, could you get off the first exit after the border crossing...there's an ATM in Blaine and I just got to fill up on some cash."

It was an unusually cold night for the time of year, and Rachel, sitting in the back seat next to Benn in his car seat, pulled up his checkered blanket. Benn held on to that wherever he went, and although asleep, his little hand seemed to pull it up tautly.

When Jack inserted his bank card into the ATM, it spewed back faster than its insertion, with the words from the screen reading colder than the night itself: "UNABLE TO PROCESS DUE TO INSUFFICIENT FUNDS."

Jack knew that there must be a technical malfunction, and reinserted the card. Another technical malfunction, he thought, as the screen read the same message with the card spewing out once again. He knew from checking his account before he'd left for Vancouver there was a few thousand dollars in it, so this made no sense whatsoever.

As Jack walked with a forlorn frown on his face toward the car, Tom shouted out, "You okay? You look like you just got three in the penalty box..."

"Tom, you got some quarters...I just need to let Marbry know about the backup at the border and that we are on our way."

Jack wasn't sure why his hand was shaking. He barely could get the coins in the pay phone slot.

"Marbry?"

"Jack, where are you, almost home?"

"Yes...we'll be there in less than forty minutes...I wanted to let you know Benn is sleeping."

"Okay, good...that makes things easier."

"Marbry, I just went to an ATM in Blaine, and the transaction was rejected twice...I know there's funds in there..."

Cutting Jack off in a piston-like manner, Marbry fired back, "I heard they're having technical malfunctions all over the area... why don't you check back in the morning?"

The forty-minute drive home seemed like hours. Weirdly, Jack felt like a stranger walking into his own house, with barely a hello from Marbry as she lifted Benn, putting him to bed.

The next morning Jack drove to the ATM. There was $3500 available.

A self-imposed earthquake in Jack's head had rattled the corridors of his conscience. He knew the marriage would never survive if he made the move and continued on in social services, yet was he "selling out" on his dream, his goals?

When Jack told her his decision to leave social services, there was no consoling counsel from Marbry. She actually grew terse in her comments. "It's refreshing that you finally are returning to the real world."

By the end of the year, Jack had given his notice to Ron Legion, who, for the first time, seem to really value Jack's presence.

Legion lamented, "Jack, this is a great loss to the agency, the state, and these children in need. Is there anything, anything we can do to dissuade you from leaving us?"

Jack's answer to this question could not be a truthful one, to Ron or to himself.

"I always wanted to try the sales world, and I have an opportunity."

Ironically, answering an ad in the *Seattle Times*, Jack garnered a sales position for Weyerhauser. The company was an environmentally responsible one with a great history of ecologically based forestry operations. They audited all their own environmental practices and seemed to have a sense of accountability and concern for their employees. In his interview, Jack was impressed with the affability of the employees. If he was going to go corporate, a seemingly accountable corporation like this would be the one to go to. Jack would be in sales in the company's paper division. There would be a 401(k), an impressive salary/commission incentive package, and a nice merit vacation scale.

Five years into the job, some romance had returned to Marbry and Jack's life. The job switch took a dead weight off his shoulders.

It seemed not too long ago that Marbry could only see magic between Jack and her. He blamed himself for bringing her not only to a place that was far from her home, but also a place that, although part of his dreams, was very distant to her dreams and desires. His feelings and attraction for Marbry never wavered, even in the worst of times they shared. He had every reason to believe life and Marbry would continue with the harmonious sense he thought he felt.

On an early spring Saturday morning the comfort of that sense of calm would depart and perhaps never return. It was late morning and Marbry, still "working only weekends" at the nursery, had left for work. The fog coming off the bay seemed to hang like a silent helicopter overhead. Jack was getting Benn's brand-new street hockey gear out of the shed when he noticed an older man walking on the front porch, peering through the first-floor bay windows. Walking up the steps, Jack realized it was Art Lowenthal.

"Mr. Lowenthal, how are you?"

"Good, Jack…you got a moment to talk?"

"Sure…everything all right?"

"Well, Jack, we have been trying to get ahold of you for a while now, and we wanted to do it in confidence. Marbry…well, has she spoken to you about her problem?"

"Marbry?" Jack answered puzzled. "No, why?" Jack's stomach was now burning with acid that was dripping in his gut like coffee beans in a roaster.

"Jack, we have given her a final warning—she was found twice stealing money from our cash register."

"Mr. Lowenthal, I am sorry—I mean, I am stunned, I am sorry, let me repay you right away."

"Jack, that won't be necessary; we settled with her. It was a good deal of cash. The first time we were privy to this unfortunate situation we couldn't account for exactly how much and why funds were missing. The second time we had to have a video installed, and, well, we let her know we had evidence of her doing this. She was upset—she did apologize, and she had her uncle from New York wire in the money…but, Jack, I think there is a bigger issue here."

Still stunned, Jack couldn't do anything but listen.

"Quite frankly, we are basically a family operation and we don't really hire outside of the family that often, but we had no reason not to trust her, and we got a great feeling from you… We had to relegate her to weekends because it's so busy and with people around…you understand."

Art Lowenthal kept speaking, yet at this point, Jack heard little of it.

All he could say was, "Art, I am so sorry…what can I do to repay you?"

"Well, as I said the money has been returned, but we wanted you to know—we didn't think you knew—but if it happens again she can't stay. It's a shame because we all like Marbry, and we can't understand it…she is like family to my wife, but there seems to be a problem there… Are you folks in an okay place financially?"

His last words were particularly hard to swallow.

"Art, we are financially in the best situation we ever have been in. I'm not certain what has happened…"

"Thanks, Jack…I'd better be getting back now. I feel a lot better that I spoke with you."

He had been pondering it for a long time, but something inside of Jack told him that he had nothing to lose by taking Cooper up on his offer of a few years ago to talk. This was the time.

It wasn't easy to track him down. Marbry spoke little of him, Christiana seemed to loathe him, and he was virtually nonexistent to the rest of the "Wellington clan."

Cooper was the salutatorian of his class at Queen's University of Kingston, and was currently a geologist for one of Canada's largest natural gas companies out in Calgary.

"Jack, Jack McKenna, Morgan's Jack? Why, I'm touched. How ARE YOU!?"

"Cooper, I have been meaning to speak with you for a while...but this isn't easy for me..."

"Jack, let it out...as we say here, 'What happens in Calgary, stays in Calgary!'"

Jack, perhaps poisoned by the others, always felt Cooper quite "odd," but something deep inside of him told him he really was the most genuine Wellington.

Jack and Cooper spoke for a good hour until Cooper had to leave for a "field assignment."

Cooper made him feel at ease immediately.

"Jack, we know, well I know, by that craaazy look in your eyes when I first met you, that you truly love my sister...but it's not all that it seems, brother."

"What's not all that it seems?"

"Jack...Mother is the king and the queen...one must pay homage to her, and pay homage to her often...I'm not sure you caught that script?!"

"Gee, I thought I just had to ask her about her favorite scenic views!"

"Huh?" Cooper ejaculated.

"Oh, it's something Marbry once told me when she was staying in the 'Pearl Guest Room.'"

"Jack, you are too puzzling to them. You are driven by something other than money, business, and accumulation of things...they are really confounded by that, and you. Oh, but

I do have to tell you, Jack, that there was much concern in my dear, dear family that you were, well, you were not 'of the faith.'"

"With all due respect, Cooper, I am not Catholic, but are they of the faith?"

"Jack, you and I both know not in practice, but in style, Jack, STYLE. That's the Quebec way—well, that's not very fair, but it's the WELLINGTON way! Jack, I couldn't have gotten any FARTHER away from my family and still have been in Canada, now, could I have… Why do you think I'm out here in the western wilderness…the prairies? I could use a little culture and comfort, you know…but you can pick your friends, but you can't pick your family!"

"I have heard that before."

"I'm most certain you have. Jack, if you didn't know already, you ought to know by now…my dear sister Morgan never wrote a check, drove a car, telephoned a man until she met you! Why, I'm not sure she ever dated… She had many formal dinners with men…oh yes…oh dear… There was that one horrifying experience she had with that golfer from the States."

"Horrifying experience?"

"Well, yes…Millicent and Wellington were in Europe. Morgan was working as a hostess at the Canadian Open at the Royal Montreal Golf Club… She met him… He was handsome in, I guess, the roughneck sort of way. Not too much later Morgan went to visit him at his college in Illinois…I found this out later…you know, Jack…I think he took advantage of Morgan…I came home for Christmas and Morgan was never the same…Mother told me not to ask any questions."

"I never knew this."

"Jack, I didn't think you did. I never saw Morgan happy again until the day you walked in...since you were the first man Morgan was with since the golfer, Mother, being Mother, naturally confused you as a golfer; that was really the Wellington signal that 'here we go again!' I knew you were genuine, so did Ed, and I think Cousin Tina...when you left, ole Tina said something to the effect of, 'Well, he's a pauper all right...but he has gentleman eyes'... That's a world-class compliment from Cousin Tina, you ought to know.

"Jack...bear with little Morgan... She's like a lost kitten out there in the Western U.S. I'm sure it's not financial... She is just needy right now... You were the 'knight in shining armor,' after all, that took her far away from the grips of our evil sister Christiana and Uncle Trent... Jack...sooo good to talk to you... I have to go... Please don't be a stranger..."

Before he could explain that he was not so sure that Marbry was "away from the grips of Christiana and Trent," Cooper was off the receiver.

Diversion

THE CONVERSATION WITH COOPER WAS not only important but reaffirming to Jack that he was not the cause of some dysfunctional if not criminal behavior on the part of Marbry.

"Who is this person? Who is this person?" The question kept nagging at Jack.

The cryptic checks to the grocery store, the vanishing money from the ATM checking account, now this? Stealing from the Lowenthals? Where was this money going?

Luckily, there was a message from Bennett on the machine that Priscilla and he were back from Albuquerque.

Jack called Bennett and Bennett's enthusiasm was effusive as ever.

"Jack, we're stoked... After Kona and our training this winter...we feel invincible... Not only that, *Runner's World* is planning to do a feature on us this spring and Priscilla's modeling is in high demand. We are moving up to Santa Cruz, and we plan to be doing a lot of traveling on the 'circuit' over the summer and fall, but mark your calendar for late February next year, that's the date for our wedding."

"That's great, Bennett."

"Jack...I'm sorry, just a little excited... How are you?"

"Bennett, a little less celebratory than you!"

"Jack, speak to me."

Ninety minutes later Jack was off the phone, and he felt a sense of relief to have a friend that he could confide in with something that to Jack was an "embarrassing personal disgrace." Bennett, always taking the high road, always giving the others the benefit of the doubt, offered, "Jack, maybe it's a bad case of homesickness… She's a great girl, just let her talk. Just remember, Jack, you're an incurable romantic and we are both fighters… things will work out."

It stuck like putty in his mind: Jack remembered that the last time they spoke Bennett had said, "WE are both romantics."

By the time Jack was able to confront Marbry with everything, he had spoken to the grocery-store manager and the nail-shop manager. The grocery-store manager had Marbry on his radar, as he'd witnessed her writing out checks in an amount usually three times the amount of the groceries, and requesting the rest in cash. He asked Jack candidly, "Does your wife have a drug issue?" He referred Jack to the nail-shop manager because one of the girls who worked at his store had heard the gossip about "the woman who was bouncing checks there." It turned out to be Marbry. Nail-shop gossip travels fast even in a city where women pride themselves on their independence and "considerate civility." Speaking with both Bennett and Cooper was cathartic, and it enabled Jack to "go easy" approaching this troubling and bizarre behavior with Marbry.

Jack got a babysitter, telling Marbry it was "date night."

They ate quietly at the Horseshoe Café, not a favorite of Marbry's, but Jack knew it would be a quiet spot and he could fortify himself with a couple of cocktails for courage.

Out of respect for Marbry, he also knew there would be none of her book-club or shopping girlfriends present at this less-than-glamorous bar/café.

Marbry caressed a cranberry juice and had the look of impending doom written across her forehead. How much she knew what he knew, he could only imagine.

With Marbry paralyzed in dead silence, Jack let out all that he knew, the terrible embarrassing conversation with Art Lowenthal, the bounced checks, the gossip at the nail shop. He took her wrists and looked her square in the eye and said, "Why, Marbry, why?"

Breaking down in tears, Marbry could only offer, "I'm scared, Jack, I'm scared."

"What are you scared about?"

"Jack, everything… I'm pregnant."

"Pregnant?"

"Yes, Jack…I'm pregnant."

If there was anything that could divert his natural inquisition into this money-and-thievery dilemma, that would be it.

"Why haven't you said anything?"

"Jack…I don't know…I'm just scared…I'm so sorry."

All Jack could do at this point was hold her and comfort her. The reason for the mysterious missing cash and the whole debacle at Lowenthals' would have to be left to another day, another appropriate time.

Whirlwind

JACK NEVER STOPPED TO THINK about how transcontinental his marriage was until the day Marguerite called and Jack had to explain that Marbry was "going to spend the last month of her pregnancy with her family back in Montreal, taking Benn out of first grade and allowing the nannies to homeschool him."

"Well, another chapter in the bicoastal life of the rich and the famous."

"Mom, if you knew how hard I was working and now traveling pretty much the whole West Coast... We have one income and my only vacation time will be when I go back to Montreal for the baby's delivery."

"Jack, you can only do what you can do...but remember, these are your children too."

His mother's comments were a little confusing at the time, but ones that would come back to haunt him.

Two nights before he left for Montreal he received a call from a somewhat familiar voice.

"Jack, is Marbree there?"

"Who may I ask is calling?"

"Monique…you know, I spent a weekend with you and Marbree up Nurth…I would very much like to speak to Marbree."

"Oh, Monique of the 'cinema verité' background."

"You remembered? Yes, may I speak to Marbree?"

"She's back East…in Montreal."

"Oh, so convenient…you know her uncle likes to fuck in the bed and fuck in the bank…you know, don't you?"

"Monique, maybe you want to call somebody else…I have to go now."

Before he turned in, Jack made his nightly call to Montreal.

"Marbry, remember the bikini-clad Monique from the cabin?"

"Jack, why are you thinking of her when I, your wife, am back here…are you behaving?"

After telling her about the strange phone call, Marbry was immediately dismissive.

"Many women want to be close to my uncle, especially now when he is obviously building a financial empire in New York! She's sooo beneath his dignity."

"Okay, but why is she calling us trying to get to you?"

"Jack, because of course she cannot get to my uncle…are we going to talk about that slut, or are you going to ask me about how Benn and I are faring?"

"There is a lot I want to speak to you about, Marbry. I'll save it for when I see you."

When Jack arrived in Quebec, it was easy to see that it was going to be hard to get Benn to leave his little "castle kingdom."

Millicent had a veritable playground, playhouse, and treehouse built off the rear atrium of the mansion for Benn.

Expecting Benn to run up and hug him, Jack was greeted first with, "Dad, can we take this with us, if we do have to go back?"

A few days later, Agnes-Marie was born. She had her mother's beautiful blue eyes shadowed by a tight knit of Shirley Temple-like curls. She was beautiful! This was an unusual christening, quite different from Benn's—there seemed to be more champagne and caviar than people. A well-intoxicated Christiana took the opportunity to be her sweetest self, coarsely saying, "Jack, congratulations, I hear you are finally making money... You will be moving back to a big Eastern city in that case now, I'm sure."

"It's not exactly a sentence to be living out West, Christiana."

"I suppose not for some, perhaps. Of course there is one benefit to living back East...Jack...you would know to say Louis Vuitton, not Lewis Vuitton...ha, ha...oh, apologies...I know Marbry always thought it adorable when you said it that way... She always fell for that primitive raw caveman masculinity in suitors!"

"Yes, just as you say, Christiana, that would be THE cultural benefit."

Before Marbry, Jack, Benn, and little Agnes-Marie left Montreal, Helene, her two boys, Scotty and Alex, and Rae-Ann showed up, baby gift in hand to "see the new baby and wish the family well." Helene was working for a traveling agency and the kids were growing in "leaps and bounds." The boys insisted on playing shinny with "Uncle Jack." Since their plane back was in the evening, Marbry gave her look of approval, so off went Jack with Benn, the boys, and Rae-Ann, who seemed the most excited, in tow on the one-kilometer walk to the pond. When the happy quintet headed back to the house, Marbry had stepped in to get "what Jack forgets to pack together."

"Kids, we have to wrap this up...some of us have to get a plane."

As Jack turned toward the house, he noticed a stately figure waving to the kids. Helene, waiting outside up on the hillside, glistened in her peach-and-lavender overcoat. Her appearance from far away belied the gloom on her face as the sun set behind her. She positioned herself within earshot of Jack, in a soft but imploring tone saying, "Jack...take care of Marbry and your family...please, and please protect them from Trent."

Before Jack could even digest what was said, Marbry came out, and goodbyes were exchanged.

En route to the airport, Marbry asked Jack, "What was Helene speaking to you about on the hillside?"

Jack, now protective of his own concerns, said mildly, "She is so happy how much the baby looks like you, Marbry."

Loving the Dream Chaser

JACK FINISHED HIS FIFTH YEAR with Weyerhaeuser, being named "Western Salesman of the Year." Benn was old enough now, Jack felt, to learn the rudiments of hockey. Marbry couldn't stop reminding Jack "that little Benn need not be a little Jack."

"No, he is going to play soccer, baseball, hockey, and whatever sports he wants to."

Agnes-Marie was the ideal little baby…sleeping at night, smiling during the day. She was the apple of her father's eye.

The next winter was one of Northwest Washington's coldest. Jack took to a renewed hobby available to him due to the temperatures well below freezing for a number of weeks. With new territorial responsibilities, and often coming home late at night, Jack would often drive off I-5 at Samish Way, park at Lake Padden, and pull out a little portable goal he had in his trunk for Benn and hit a puck on the frozen lake by himself. If it were not a school night he would pick up Benn first, and they would shinny on the lake for hours. Being alone with little Benn brought back memories of playing shinny with Preston and Bennett and his childhood friends on Vancouver's Trout Lake. Marbry was enjoying an aerobics class that met thrice weekly, and everything seemed good.

"Jacky, Jacky Boy." The voice was familiar...Danny McDevitt was in town. Danny was now a well-paid "consultant and recruiter for the sporting goods industry."

"The multi-billion-dollar-PROFITING sporting goods industry," as Danny would put it.

It was 7:30 p.m., and it sounded like "McD" was already three sheets to the wind. But Danny's voice on the telephone meant only one thing.

"Padden tonight?"

"As soon as Marbry comes home...I'll get over there!"

"Well, hurry it up, Jacky Boy...you don't shinny by yourself."

Jack laughed to himself as he saw a bright-red Toyota Supra Turbo parked off Valley View. It wasn't the ostentatious color of the car that marked it as Danny's but the huge hockey-stick decal with an American and Canadian flag crossing over it on the rear window.

Jack laced up, went down, and there was big Danny, screeching across the lake, "Jacky Boy...defend"...as the grey-haired bull came rambling toward him, slicing the puck between his legs.

For the next hour there was nothing but the sound of a puck "grizzling off a patch of Padden," as Jack put it, reveling in this carefree passionate existence. The beauty of this meeting under an awning of silver stars was that here were two men, one with a significant patch of grey, the other with the demeanor of a staid senator, mixing it up on the ice.

In that existential moment, Jack thought, "This is what life was supposed to be, the simplicity of sharing in the joy of what we have, what we love."

"We have to cut this good clean delayed adulthood short, Jacky Boy...I got an interesting nugget for you."

Danny "McD" always had some interesting "nuggets," and his stock tips were actually more on cue than his "motivational" sales spiels. He loved to tell how he envisioned himself as an "NHL coach," when he was hired to "retrain employees...you know, Jack...I get them to bathe in the company tub."

"Jacky Boy, let's meet down at the Waterfront on Holly."

"Danny, c'mon, not the bar where Bundy and Bianchi drank!"

"Jacky Boy, I'm sure it wasn't the only place where serial killers stopped by...besides, the bartendress, Lynne, is the best in Bellingham!"

As the suds flowed in the corner table, Danny's words seemed weighty, not frothy like his bombastic "paid-for-hire" consulting soliloquies he'd become known for. As Jack found out later, McDevitt was enjoying a meteoric rise from journeyman salesman to "one of the highest-paid consultants in the industry," according to the lead trade journal.

"Lynne," Danny called out to the hardworking, affable bar owner, "two of those Chuckanut IPAs for my man and me." It was easy to feel like family at this spot, as everyone serving not only was family, but treated their customers as such.

"Jack, I know things are good and safe for you at Weyerhauser, but I want you to hear me out tonight."

Jack knew when Danny went from calling him "Jacky Boy" to Jack, the tone and the conversation were changing to one of a serious nature.

"You are a hockey guy. You are a Canadian hockey guy with everything that means...you are hardworking, loyal, disciplined...Jack, you need to get BACK IN THE GAME."

"I think it's a little late for that!"

"Jack, I'm not talking as a player. You know how two years ago Nike bought your country's largest hockey company, Canstar/Bauer? Well, things looked promising the first two years...hey, remember the Micron Mega? Seventy percent of the NHL players were wearing that...it was a marketing dream...now the word on the street is sales are off at the company, particularly in this I-5 corridor, and they are looking for someone to jumpstart it."

McD continued, "The way I see it, there is only one man to do the job, and he's the guy who couldn't defend my shots under the moonlit sky tonight."

"Me...you got to be kidding, Danny!"

"Listen, Jack, you have all the right ingredients for this...you love the game...you always have...you know sales...you have the right connections to Canada and the States...this would be a grand slam for you!"

"This would involve work over the border as well?"

"Yes, Jack, apparently there has been some resistance to the Nike brand up in some provincial circles up North... It seems to be a slow-go for what seemed at one point to be a gold mine for Nike."

McDevitt kept pitching to Jack, "When Nike bought Canstar a couple of years ago, there was no reason to believe it wouldn't be a billion-dollar business by now. Jack, they have some great people, real hockey people in the company, but you, you were a natural leader on the ice. I know, Jack, I am your friend, but I did do my homework. I do know what you're doing for Weyerhaeuser...Jack, will you consider thinking it over and speaking to Marbs about it?"

"Danny, of course...I'll think it over."

"Good, because once I get you in, I'm going to get you to get your friend Bennett in…I can tell he's a real go-getter, love that guy…let him get that triathlon thing out of his system…love him… Is it me, or who doesn't have the greatest affection for a guy like that who's out there chasing his dream?"

Thunderstorms

Traveling most of the West, Jack had to deal with signal restrictions in some remote areas. His colleagues in the company called him the "Lone Ranger," as he was one of the last salesmen with both a car phone and one of the new developing cell phones.

Often Jack would receive rings on both lines at the same time. As he finished an important "budgetary conference call," there was an East Coast area code flashing up on his old mobile phone. It was Arne Rosenfeld. Arne was now completing his first year as the chief financial officer for a start- up investment firm right off Wall Street.

"Jack, congrats on the new child, how's Marbry and Benn?"

"They're great."

"Good…don't know if you heard…I'm engaged! Can you believe it, somebody is attracted to me…she must have the same nearsightedness Marbry has!"

"Apparently!"

"Hey, Jack, what was the name of Marbry's uncle again?"

"Trent Doertz."

"Okay, it is him…a principal in Reynolds, Carey, and Doertz out of New York?"

"Don't tell me, your buddy from Princeton over at the SEC is investigating him?"

"Nah…just noticed something that came across the financial papers this morning, and I was thinking about you."

"What was that…obviously it was something juicy if you're calling me?"

"Nah…but I remember you giving me a little about this guy…thinks he's hot stuff, if memory serves me well."

"Your memory always served you well, Arne."

"Well, anyway…just a small piece that hit me about how a Canadian woman named Monique Lavallière was suing him and the firm for cherry-picking her stock trades."

"Okay, that sounds obscene…what is cherry-picking, I know you're not referring to the cherry-picking we refer to in hockey, like loafing around the goal?"

"Exactly…it's a little more than loafing…it's a deliberate financial crime of sorts… It's, Jack, to put it mildly, a lot more roguish."

"Explain."

"It occurs when a trader like him executes trades without assigning any particular trade to a particular account, and then late in the trading day, he would assign an unprofitable trade to a disfavored account. So hers would be a discretionary or what turns out to be an unfavorable account, while he's placing the good ones with his own named accounts."

Arne continued, "It's very hard to identify, investigate, and prove."

"Wow, sounds brilliantly manipulative."

"It is, and as I said, it's very hard to investigate and prove. Doesn't sound like something the guy you described could pull off, does it?" Arne asked rather sheepishly.

"Why do you say that, Arne? It sounds totally like something he totally would do."

"Oh, I got the impression you made him out to be a loud-mouth, showy guy."

"Well, he is all that, but what does that have to do with it?"

"Well, usually these type of guys, if they are going to do something like that, tend to keep a very conservative, low profile…they would want to stay under the radar. The Feds only go after 'white-collar crime' if it's something really big, like Milken was involved in. But that guy is and was a huge philanthropist."

"Yeah, I don't see Trent Doertz funding medical research or helping humanity the way Milken did."

"You remember me telling you that?!"

All of a sudden Jack remembered Helene's ominous warnings.

"Arne, what did you say the woman's name was who's suing?"

"Monique Lavallière."

Arne sensed the pregnant pause in the conversation.

"Don't tell me you know who she is. I know Marbry is from Montreal, but Montreal is a big place?"

"Arne, you wouldn't believe me, if it's the Monique I think it is."

"Well, Jack, if he did do this, she has a snowball's chance in hell of winning the suit…R, C, & D, as they are called, have assets of over $300 million, and you know what comes with that…a lot of expensive big-time lawyers protecting their interests. Jack, are you still there?"

"I'm here."

"Hey, you are invited to the wedding…it's in June…you'll be getting an invite…it's going to be back East, here out in the Long Island Hamptons. Jack, you still there? What's that noise?"

"You would call it a thunderstorm…it's coming off the Pacific and fast."

"Jack…you heard about my invite?"

"Yes, Arne, that's great…I'm looking forward to it."

Suffering

EVERYTHING WAS A STILL PICTURE. It was a wet, windy, yet balmy early February Wednesday night when Jack walked in from a very long sales day. Marbry was at her aerobics class. Madison, their young neighbor and babysitter, wore a checkered sweater over her Mudd jeans. Her dimples twinkled when Jack handed her the money as Benn didn't move from the TV set and Agnes lay peacefully asleep. The note read, "Call Arne 202-400-9112...sounds important. xxxooo, Marbry."

"Two times in the same week, after I haven't heard from him in over a year...more questions about Trent?" Jack mused as he hung up his Patagonia shell.

Sitting down in the kitchen, Jack looked through the mail, sipping on an apple juice in his favorite pewter mug. As the rain pelted away, for some reason he knew he didn't want to call Arne back. He dialed anyway.

"Jack...Jack...Bill and Jim, they wanted to call, but they—Jack, they couldn't."

"Arne, you okay?"

"Jack, Jack—Bennett."

Jack knew by the halting hesitation of Arne's voice.

"Is he okay?"

"Jack, he's dead."

The Pewter mug was in pieces all over the kitchen. He didn't know how it got that way. Now he didn't notice anything.

"I'm staying on the phone."

They cried together over the phone. He didn't need to know how; that would only make the words more real. But it was REAL.

Bennett, on a fifty-mile training ride, heading south on Route 1 halfway between Half Moon Bay and Santa Cruz with Priscilla and two other cyclists, was hit and instantly killed when a twenty-three-year-old girl in a 1985 Toyota Corolla made an unexplained U-turn, hitting a southbound SUV. In veering off, the SUV still hit and sheared the Corolla in half, which ricocheted off, slamming Bennett and his bike head first into the guardrail. The California Highway Patrolman, in answering the distress call, couldn't distinguish which was the driver's torso and which was Bennett's. Passerby drivers stopped and rushed out of their cars. They could sense the distress of the officer, who was in apparent shock, seeing the residue of an accident he had never before witnessed in his twenty-eight years on the force. The innocent family in the SUV was driving within the speed limit, returning from a President's Day visit to the San Francisco Zoo.

The driver was working as a nanny in Santa Cruz, and, from the investigation later, when the cell phone was found in the road fifty meters from the accident, had answered a call that somehow prompted her to take the immediate, impulsive turn. The SUV was carrying a mother, her mother, and three children. The oldest boy was medevacked to the Stanford University Medical Center. A saintly woman visiting from New York had pulled over with her husband and placed jackets and blankets over the children, their mother, and a bruised but shocked Priscilla. The two other cyclists, lagging just a hundred meters behind Bennett, escaped with minor bruises from braking fast. Before the bevy of EMTs and additional CHP arrived, one of the passersby, checking for ID to notify the next of kin, noticed a bulge coming from the key pocket of what they now could distinguish as the cyclist. It was a picture of a little boy. That boy was "little Bennett," Benn.

It was the worst day of Jack's life. Bennett, the dreamer, the romantic, the fighter, was gone.

So, it seemed, was Jack for a long while.

Jack never left the kitchen. When Marbry came home, Benn had gotten up and told her, "Mommy I think somebody died." It was the first time Jack had seen her cry like that, genuine tears, since their days at McGill. There would be much to do before the funeral plans were made, but for the McKennas, the funeral had started.

The next morning calls were coming in by the droves. Jack couldn't talk. Perhaps it was the night of emptying the bourbon bottle that he somehow found, never knowing before that it existed in his house. A gift for his Fourth of July party left over from a few years back. It was the first time ever that Jack had imbibed hard liquor. He couldn't stop hearing the specter of Bennett's laughs. Calm wasn't to be found now in his genome.

Marbry reluctantly took the phone calls. As almost impossible as it seemed for Jack to talk to anyone, it seemed an unnatural burden of sheer sadness for Marbry to do so. The only evocative emotion Jack had seen from Marbry was the romance once so flowered in their relationship. Like the luster of the cherry blossoms in Montreal, so vivid, yet so fleeting, that crispness had now abated. This tragedy seemed to rekindle a distant horror that would be too much for Marbry to revisit.

Marbry would stay home with Agnes-Marie and Benn for the funeral. This would be too much for the children, still too young to bear it. Jack had mused that perhaps Benn would be old enough to understand. Marbry, for better or worse, convinced him otherwise. Jack would drive up with Tom and RB again to Vancouver. Along with everything else that was bombarding his mind, Jack mused that Marbry's absence, even if practical, was foreboding.

There was never a wedding, nor a funeral, where St. Ann's Cathedral had seen such a crowd. With Bennett's mother passing away just a few years prior, his much-older sister and cousins were his only blood relatives alive. Jack, Uncle Mac, and Marguerite knew long ago they were the "family" who Bennett would come home to. However, in addition to the literally hundreds of Team Canada athletes and friends that Bennett made over the years who were present, there was another family in attendance. There were several dozen young people wearing bright-blue polo shirts with an insignia on the left chest that read "Cyclists Serving Others." On the back of their shirts were the bold adjectives in bright-red lettering outlined in white, "Love," "Sacrifice," "Serve." This was a group, Jack knew, who clearly had more than a connection to Bennett.

Jack, a pallbearer, gave the eulogy, stopping three times to contain his emotions. Of the other pallbearers, two were his Villanova teammates, two were his Team Canada teammates, and then there was Mac. After the service, Mac whispered to Marguerite, "Margs, I haven't met this kind of sorrow in my gut in over fifty years." At the cemetery among the throng of grieving friends and admirers, Jack noticed somebody he wouldn't really expect to see there.

It was Helene, formerly Doertz, now going by her maiden name of Lemeuix.

Politely beckoning Jack over to where they were standing, Helene, eyes teared, mustered, "Jack, I am sooo sorry for your loss…we know how much Bennett meant to you, your family."

"Helene, I'm overwhelmed… How did you find out, how did you get here?"

"Addie saw it in the papers, and told me, and I called Marbry, and understanding how she must be with the children, I felt that the women in our family should be represented and be there for you in your grief… Addie was kind to see me off safely at the airport…you know there are gentlemen in the Wellington family."

Jack knew she could only be referring to Addison and Cooper.

"Well, Marguerite, my mother, is having a gathering after the funeral mass at our family house."

"Jack, that's so kind of you, but it would not be appropriate for me to be there without Marbry… I have a flight out at five, and already your friend Arne and his lovely fiancée are kind enough to give me a ride."

After the burial, Jack made sure to go over and talk to Arne first. When he thanked Arne for coming to the funeral, Arne looked a tad indignant. "He was one of the best human beings I ever encountered…I wouldn't think of not coming. Did Bill tell you about those kids in the blue shirts?"

"No, not yet."

"Well, as you could have guessed, that was Bennett's creation. It started out when he did volunteer work in Surrey."

"Bennett?"

"Yes, he was going to get you involved but he knew with the wedding and the baby and all you needed to focus on, now was not the time. So when Priscilla and he were starting to cash in on their triathloning, he made it bigger, donating his own time and money when he was in B.C., cajoling and garnering bike manufacturers to sponsor, and it grew to an organization where street kids, doing volunteer work, would earn bikes...and they weren't cheap bikes, by any means, Jack."

Jack, looking toward the heavens, blurted out, "Bennett, how did our lives get apart?"

Arne, realizing the regret he was creating in Jack, retorted, "Jack, it's important for you to know he had dreams of you and him making this a North American organization."

"But why?" Jack continued.

"Jack, he told me things you were confronting...that's why I called you when I did...Bennett was very concerned what was happening, and what he felt Marbry's uncle was doing!"

"What was that?"

"Jack, now is not the time for this, we are both losing perspective here..."

"Well, you are coming over to my mother's, I trust?"

"Jack...we have a flight back...we are driving Helene."

"Yes, I know...you all are very special..."

"Jack, we'll talk again...love you, man!"

Marguerite had a gathering after the burial back at the house in Delbrook. Literally hundreds of people brought food, gathering inside and outside the small three-bedroom house. When Jack walked back in, he noticed immediately the picture that somehow his mother dug up, standing prominently in a polished frame on the living room mantle, a picture he hadn't seen in over twenty years. It was Bennett, Preston, and Jack, the three of them holding hockey sticks with the Canadian flag etched prominently across each of them, all wearing T-shirts with one word across them, "GRIND."

Jack again recognized the grace in his mother, for too early in her life had she buried a husband, and now she was burying a young man whom she looked upon as her third son.

Aftermath

WHEN ALMOST EVERYBODY WAS GONE from the gathering, Mac announced that he would like to take a short ride over to Stanley Park. Marguerite encouraged Jack to go with his uncle, understanding that there wouldn't be time in the near future for either to be able to do so. Mac was mellowing in his later years and Jack was eager to listen and spend some time with somebody who, in his own way, always cared about others.

Though it was late winter, the snow crocuses were like little yellow Martians sneaking out from the ground. The alluring fragrance of sweetbox and the vines of evergreen clematis were intoxicating in and around Stanley Park. Walking in silence along the seawall for what seemed like several kilometers, the pair came upon the plaque near Siwash Rock honoring the man who dedicated his career to the building of this beautiful walkway.

Jack spoke first. "They say this one guy dedicated his life to the masonry of this seawall."

"Yes, no exaggeration. Even in his dying days, Jimmy Cunningham would come out to take a look at the progress of it."

"You know, Uncle Mac, sometimes I feel like I reacted rebelliously too fast...the thought of committing a life, a career, to one task...I thought maybe I could do several things, and pursue them well...it really hasn't worked out the way I thought... Bennett seemed to have that singular focus and it was working out for him, yet I found out he also was creating things to help others…I just wish I had spent more time with him…he always seemed to have it together."

"Don't be hard on yourself… Nobody misunderstood your intentions, Jack."

That one line coming from Mac was as salving a solace as the mist from the Salish Sea.

"Thanks, Uncle Mac."

Before Jack could continue, Mac went on, "Jack…I noticed the sadness in your eyes before Bennett died…you always carried the weight of the family…you know I came on strong to your older brother when your dad died…I tried too hard to be the proper patriarchal figure, I guess…and what did your brother do…he said piss off…rejected everything and went his own way…and fast… You, you took things to heart…you felt you were going to create an empire for us, yourself, and lord, who knows who else… Jack, you tried too hard…but there's no sin in that. Believe me, Jack, I wasn't the perfect father figure, but I did try, and I did learn to listen…and, Jack, I've had to change!"

"When was that, Uncle Mac?" Jack said sheepishly.

"Well, longer ago than you might believe. Listen, Jack, back in the late fifties when the Canadian's goalie Jacques Plante wore that protective mask, when nobody else did, we all thought he was a 'pussy.' Pussy, my ass! He played with that thing all the way to a Stanley Cup! He was the smart one…he was the bold one…. he was the man ahead of his time…it takes some men, myself included, to take a step back and figure out somebody who we might think is crazy is starting a revolution. Remember around the time you were asking my friend Angus to contact his brother in Connecticut…you know what Angus said to me?"

"What did he say, Uncle Mac?"

"'Mac, I'm so glad you're letting your boys create their own lives...they need a father figure, not a Canadian John Wayne... Angus—can you believe HE said that to me?!'"

Waxing more sentimental, Mac spoke on. "Angus was the one who got me to come around after your aunt Elizabeth died...I guess I was like a zombie for quite a while... One day Angus says to me, 'Mac, cut the crap...wipe the sadness from your eyes, and live the way Elizabeth would have wanted you to live.' You know, Jack, Angus would've been a great hockey star as well. He once shared with me this lesson he learned about focus his coach taught his teammates and him when he played in the Juniors."

"What was that?"

"His coach once had the guys take a filled water cup in practice and skate around the rink four times without letting any water spill out."

"What was the point of that?"

"Exactly, Jack, that was my question. But apparently he asked the players if they thought about anything else as they were doing it. Apparently not a player on the team thought of anything else but keeping the water in the cup during the drill. He told them, 'That's the way you should exist on the ice and in life always...not letting any other distractions destroy your concentration, your focus.' Angus told me, 'That's what you've got to do, Mac, concentrate on all you have to live for.'"

"That guy sounds like a great coach and Angus sounds like a great friend."

"We only need one good one, Jack, to keep us honest and real. You know, Jack, I'm sure you're finding, as young as you are, that there are three reasons you begin to lose friends over the course of the years: one, your fault, you become too selfish; two, their fault, they become too selfish; or three, which is the one that happens to most people—life gets in the way...people have families and careers and you realize how little time is left for everything else.

"Jack...I know what you are feeling with the loss of Bennett... but I believe, and I know you in your heart believe, it was the third reason that you guys fell somewhat apart...you were just caught up in life and living...neither of you two were ever in the ballpark of being selfish or inconsiderate to each other."

"I miss him, and I miss talking with him about something that is very important to me..." Jack muffled.

"Jack, that could only be your wife and family," Mac answered.

"Yeah, Marbry...she just seemed like everything I thought was important in a woman...intelligent, beautiful, respectful, understanding, interesting..." Jack started to trail off.

"Jack, you're not speaking in the past tense, are you, or are you?"

Mac was only going to let Jack speak to his hunches...and Jack did.

He told Mac of the strange missing money and the even stranger responses from Marbry.

"Jack, I know you thought I was a hockey zealot...and selfishly wanted you to be our next great B.C. hockey hero, but the fact was you WERE...look at the incredible influence you had on the next great players from B.C...Bruce Courtnall, Doug Lidster, Craig Redmond, NHL players and great men... but more importantly, you took the courage you learned from the game and used it in your ideals...but the greatest respect I have for you is you never gave up...you aren't giving up...Jack, understand I have great respect for Marbry…but the weight of the world was placed on you marrying a girl like that from a family like that…and you never even thought twice about it… you just moved ahead…and you have to keep moving ahead… things will work out."

Mac smiled his great smile, his weathered wrinkles bringing in the wisdom of his years.

"Despite living down in the OTHER country, you have the heart of a Canadian lion…and I'm damn proud of you."

It was dark now, and as they walked back on the pathway one could still see the white of the blooming "snowdrops," the flowers Marguerite had always called the harbingers of spring.

Deafening Sounds

MARBRY WASN'T VERY GOOD WITH tragedy. She went from overdone solemnity to comments bordering on shallow. She seemed lost in some unknown space, as some of her comments didn't really make much sense.

"Jack, you have to get yourself going, Bennett would have wanted the best for you." Perhaps the latter quote was necessary, as Jack had graduated to having a little Jack Daniels every night, which added weight to both his waistline and his getting up in the mornings.

Jack buried himself in his work for the time being, but he was already contemplating the change he knew he had to make. He had gathered himself to tell Marbry about his consideration of Danny McDevitt's offer.

Her initial response was resentful, so he backed off considering it or talking about it. At this point he thirsted for some harmony.

The hope of Mac's words fostered itself in Benn and Agnes-Marie. Benn was starting to show his dad's athletic prowess and seemed to be particularly fast on or off the ice. His acceleration instincts were as quick on the ice as they were on a soccer field. Jack was reveling in the growth of them both. Agnes-Marie had sculpted a particular personality that seemed beyond her two years.

Davis Hughson, the McKennas' gregarious and most favorite neighbor, had been moving swiftly up the ladder with his lumber-brokering firm, and had moved his wife, Kelly, and three-year-old twins to Mercer Island. That summer Davis threw a "Salmon Days" party at his new, elaborate home, complete with a built-in pool. It was time for Agnes-Marie to try out the new white-trimmed red bathing suit Jack had bought her that summer. As Benn held his younger sister's hand in the shallow side of the Hughsons' trumpet-shaped pool, Jack stretched out his arms toward Agnes-Marie to come to him. Since she took her time, "Daddy" swam toward her. As he came closer, she looked at him with a scowl, and joined in his arms. While he hugged her, bobbing her up and down in the blue sunlit pool water, Agnes-Marie proceeded to grab tautly her daddy's chest hair, causing Jack to writhe in pain at the temporary discomfort his beautiful little daughter created. Everybody at poolside screamed with laughter. It was clear that even at this young age, Agnes-Marie was one strong-minded, independent young girl.

It was the first time in a few months Jack had been able to get the family out together with friends and really enjoy their company and the outdoors. Davis had enjoyed meeting Jack's cousin Tom so much when he was up visiting Jack and Marbry years earlier that he and Tom had kept up a close friendship. Davis invited him and Rachel to the party. Tom had advised Davis on environmental issues concerning lumber cuts, so the relationship was more than just that of mere acquaintances. Rachel, in her faded bandana and cut-off short denim shorts, caught the disapproving eye of the highbrow wives at the party; conversely, her alluring natural scarlet hair caught the approving eye of the men present. Their "approval" was noticed when she stripped down to her bikini, revealing a toned, curvaceous body with a tattoo on her back outlining a female figurine yielding a guitar with "RB" blazed across it. Davis seemed to know more about the significance of the "RB" tattoo.

Excitingly telling Jack, Davis shouted, "Have you gone to see Tom and Rachel in any of the clubs in Seattle?"

"Not yet," Jack replied as both he and Marbry watched with interest how Rachel was able to take Agnes-Marie further out in the pool, well beyond where Jack had lost valuable pieces of chest hair.

"Well, you ought to…there's a whole incredible music scene going on over there…and I'm telling you, Jack, it's beyond Nirvana and Pearl Jam…and Tom and Rachel's band is the bomb."

Jack, turning to his pale, always schoolbookish-looking cousin, implored, "Don't tell me you are a full-fledged grunge now?"

"Jack, we like to think of ourselves as an eclectic alternative band," Tom said proudly.

"We're playing at the Sit and Spin on the fourth next Friday and Saturday, and the Velvet Elvis the following weekend… you and Marbry should come…Rachel has a seventeen-year-old sister…she could babysit the kids."

"You guys have to go see them, Jack," Davis chimed in. "RB and the Blasters are going to be big, I'm telling you."

With Agnes-Marie out of the pool and Benn still in playing water polo with the other kids, Marbry whispered to Jack, "Imagine having our kids babysat by her sister? And could you put down that drink, you haven't even eaten yet!"

Jack quickly complied.

As Davis started to grill the salmon, the clear sky radiated the peak of Mt. Rainier, which stood behind the eastern vista of the rooftop as if it were guarding the supremacy of the region.

The day was a needed one for the family—or so Jack thought, but the joy was brought to a halt as on the drive back home Marbry reminded Jack of her priorities.

Benn was busy counting the cars they drove by and Agnes-Marie was fast asleep.

Marbry insisted, "Well, Jack, you have to be impressed—our old neighbor who at one time was moving shit buckets is now living in a palatial house on Mercer Island."

"Shit buckets…wow, Marbs, you have a better memory than I give you credit for."

"Conversely, nothing personal, but seriously, your cousin Tom and his girlfriend…some of your family members just can't seem to grow up!"

Jack answered in a bothered, yet puzzled tone, "Tom always wanted to be a musician, that was his dream…I didn't hear him talk about work, so it sounds like, as Davis says, it's going really well."

"What, his band?" Marbry rifled back.

"Yeah, his band and his life…I'm happy it's going real well for them…I think we should go down and hear them play!"

"Jack, you can't be serious, you should be discouraging your cousin from that stuff, the way your brother wants to discourage you from the silly things you are doing out in this God-forsaken place!"

"Silly things…my brother…this God-forsaken place?"

"Yes, I've been speaking to Preston…he's concerned about you."

"Is he? Well, how come he hasn't spoken to me about it?!"

"He doesn't think you would listen. He thinks, I'm certain, that you changing fields again would be as silly as what I think about your cousin and his crazy music interests."

Since the death of Bennett, Jack had been trying to read a lot of inspirational books. There was one quote that resonated with him, and he made sure to write it down in his day planner. It was a Chinese proverb that said, "The person who says it cannot be done should not interrupt the person who is doing it."

As Marbry babbled on, Jack murmured that quote to himself.

Benn was now asleep. They were almost home, and Marbry, looking out the window, said, "You're not even listening to me."

Movement

"JACK, IT'S ARNE."

Jack was so glad to hear the sound of his voice for the first time since Bennett's funeral. As strong and true as Mac's words that "you really only need one friend" were, Jack knew he was blessed with more than one true friend. But with the absence of Bennett, Arne seemed to be the voice of friendship that Jack both needed and yearned for.

"I'm just calling to remind you that all you need to do is to get your and Marbry's plane ticket to Kennedy... We'll have a car waiting for you under 'Rosenfeld party' and we are putting you and Marbry up in one of the Hamptons' suites at our expense... we are really looking forward to all this."

Jack felt, in a perverse way, since the wedding was back East and a "socially prominent crowd" was sure to be present, Marbry could find little fault with the crowd or her time with Jack. It was an event she could happily brag to her sister Christiana about.

Between the time he took off for Bennett's funeral and this wedding, Jack would have exhausted his "personal days" at Weyerhaeuser. He'd also exhausted his contemplations on career change. He was going to contact Danny, and if, after all these months, he would still consider and recommend him for the Canstar position, he would take it. His last job move was for Marbry, and despite his "moving" for her, she remained unmoved. This move was going to be for him and his mental and emotional happiness, thus ultimately for his family's benefit. If it all worked out, he would announce the news to Marbry after Arne and Lara's wedding and she would accept it more readily.

He was going to wait no longer. Jack called Danny.

"Jacky Boy...good to hear from you...how have you been doing? ...I wanted to give you some time after Bennett's death, but I need now to bring up one more time that subject we spoke about."

"Danny, is it still available?

"For you, Jacky Boy, greater than ever."

Jack heaved a huge sigh of relief. Everything again, Jack believed, could be scripted together well...and the timing was impeccable.

Marbry had resigned from Lowenthals' and to Jack, her reasoning was logical. Marbry expressed that the "kids were getting too big and I would like to be at Benn's soccer games on weekends too." She seemed to love her "book-club meetings," and with the city of Bellingham burgeoning a honeycomb of trails around the city, she would go on walks with a couple of friends from the neighborhood. In their younger days at McGill, Jack would marvel how Marbry could eat all the sugar-loaded sweets at the sundry French bakeries that surrounded them, and not gain a pound. The thirties had not accorded her with such blessings, and she grew self-conscious. To Jack, she was just as alluring with or without the extra pounds, or, as she would call it, "extra softness." With the long walks, however, she regained her beautiful figure, and what appeared to be their love life.

A few days before flying to Arne's wedding, Marbry told Jack that she would like to fly Benn and Agnes-Marie back to see and stay with Millicent and Walter, and then fly to New York, joining Jack for the wedding. She said, "Millicent and my father are paying for the trip and flight." It seemed like a good plan, and Marbry seemed happy.

Jack only found out later that Benn and Agnes-Marie would be staying for the rest of the summer in Montreal.

Arne and Lara's wedding was as beautiful and plush and inviting as only two kind, yet very ambitious, successful Wall Street financiers could make it.

Arne, seemingly the energy and brain of every room he ever walked into, took a backseat to the very elegant and equally brilliant Lara, née Schweitzer, Rosenfeld. The wedding was held at the Hamptons' "Blue Stream," a classic country club known for not only its prestigious membership, but also its eighteen-hole golf course, which swept down to the ocean, stopping at the members' beach club. In many places on the eastern end of Long Island, resorts and clubs had trended toward the tacky and the terrible, placating the "nouveau riche" of the eighties and nineties. The "Stream," as it was most known, retained its classic old-world flavor with stunning new-world amenities. The clean white paint of the boardwalk on the beach, adjacent to the golf course, glistened at night under the stars, which glittered in the shadows of the cute cabanas members enjoyed.

It was throwback music to Jack's ears when Marbry looked into his eyes and said, "This is the most beautiful wedding I've ever been to since ours, Jack, at the University Club." The wedding was magnificent, the dancing was rhythmic, and the feeling, so long missing, had reappeared in their nights together here on Long Island's "east end."

Like a sunny day turning into a rainy downpour, that "throwback music" proved to be fleeting when they arrived back at SeaTac airport. As they drove home, a trickle of rain drizzled on the windshield. Celine Dion's "Power of Love" bellowed on KISW, and to Jack nothing could be a greater omen than to tell Marbry his decision then and now!

When Jack told Marbry of his intention of leaping careers, "for the long-term future of our family," it was like he'd released the trigger of a stun gun, shooting her in the heart.

Celine Dion's lyrics of love apparently no longer resonating with her, Marbry, turning off the station with violent force, blurted, "How could you?"

Once again, Jack read Marbry, and the mood, wrong.

Clueless

JACK TOOK THE CANSTAR POSITION and his introduction to the company couldn't have been more exciting. The Nike magic was apparent and alive in his introduction to the company at the first meeting in Portland. It was a blend of high-energy seminars revealing the creative marketing plans, reviewing the product line, and reminiscing about hockey days with the strong mix of old hockey guys in the sales forces. Jack hadn't been so charged up since his visit to Connecticut to witness the smooth and successful structure of the Mt. St. John School.

The speakers alone were phenomenal. The sales force was treated to an awe-inspiring lecture by former collegiate basketball player, now a Nike vice-president, known around Nike circles as "H," the great Howard White. They laughed hilariously as one of the global executives from the running department, Fred Doyle, told his story from the perspective of a young athlete, field representative, and now executive. They walked around in the corporate park where the buildings were named after the great athletes who wore the product, such as Steve Prefontaine, Dan Fouts, John McEnroe, Alberto Salazar, Joan Benoit-Samuelson, Bo Jackson, and others. On their tour, Jack mused to Danny McDevitt, "Before I'm finished with this company, there's going to be a deserving Canadian hockey player up there on one of those buildings."

"That's the spirit, Jacky Boy...they're gonna love ya here," Danny chimed in.

Jack knew he wouldn't have to create a revolution like he'd attempted in social services; Nike had already created the athletic revolution. It was hard not to embrace the electricity that effused from his new endeavor. Driving the five hours back to Bellingham, Jack wore the special hockey jersey the company had made for the sales force. "Coquitlam," his old team, was emblazoned across the front, and his old number, "32," on the back.

He could now do away with his old ax-heavy mobile phone, as the company provided the latest cellular phones to its force.

Midway through his drive up I-5, the old mobile phone rang in what, Jack reflected, was possibly the last call he would receive on this dinosaur. It was Cooper.

"Jack...did I get you at a good time?"

"Sure, Coop, let me put you on the speaker; I'm driving the freeway back from Portland."

"Oh, yes, I heard the rumblings about the career change."

Cooper could have told him that Walter and Millicent wanted Jack shot, and it wouldn't have fazed Jack after his supercharged day in Portland.

"Oh, I'm sure that's what they were...rumblings, as you say..."

"Well, you know the Wellingtons always fear change...but let me not overstate the obvious. I wanted to see how things with you and Morgan are doing...I'm sure we'll have at least a little time to chat at Christiana's wedding."

"Wedding, what...when is that?"

"Oh, dear me, Morgan keeps everything from you, doesn't she now?!"

"I'm sure I'll get the full info as to when we have to be in Montreal, but when is it? I'm just starting this new job, and I don't want to create rumblings elsewhere!"

"Understood…September."

"Oh, great…is it that fellow Monroe?"

"Jack, you ARE much too kind…don't you mean to say 'that nitwit Monroe'?"

Laughing, Jack muttered, "I'm glad you are going to be there, Coop!"

"Jack, they have been living together for years…of course Mother doesn't condemn that situation…do you know he was nothing but a grocery clerk at one of the old Dominion stores before Trent somehow got him in the car sales business?"

"Did that come with the Porsche he drives?"

"Yes, it does seem rather strange, doesn't it? Not only that, Jack, but Monroe is a veteran with the nose candy…I happen to be privy to a funny but true story I have on good authority of why he was fired from his first car company selling his used Chryslers."

"Got to hear it."

"Well, apparently he had some tardy and no-show days at work. One day the GM calls him in and says to him, 'Monroe, it won't affect our relationship at all, but I have to ask you something, are you doing coke?' Monroe answers back, 'Only sometimes!' The GM then tells him, 'Okay, I thought so…you're fired!'"

Laughing, Jack shrieked, "Couldn't have happened to a nicer guy…isn't this latest one the fourth car company he's with?"

"Jack, I think it's actually five…"

"Where did you hear that from…the good authority wasn't Addie, was it?"

"Yes, and I'm worried about him, Jack."

"Why?"

"Oh, heavens, Jack, you ARE naive. Can't you see we Wellingtons deal with Mother's controlling nature and Father's deviancy in our very own ways...I left the 'nest'; Christiana wants to control everything and everybody, that's why the clueless Monroe is perfect for her; Morgan, well, Morgan, you know more than me on that, and Addie, the most honest soul of us, is having a drug issue."

"Is there anything I can do? Can I speak to him?"

"Jack, you ARE a beautiful man; if I were heterosexual, I would have gone after you before Morgan, but seriously, yes, if you get his ear at the wedding, he respects you, and I did want you to know that!"

"I appreciate that, Cooper!"

"Jack, most important, GET WITH IT, for heaven's sake... we'll speak at the wedding...but I think now more than ever, you should watch your back with the Wellingtons!"

"Cooper, thanks!"

It seemed to be an ominous warning from a trusted source, but Jack let his charged-up enthusiasm from the experience earlier in the day obscure his cluelessness.

Foreclosure

Labor Day had come and gone, and the kids were both in school. Benn was entering the fifth grade, and Agnes-Marie was entering kindergarten.

Autumn, with or without the leaves coloring in the Northwest, always ushered in a sense of change. The air was a little cooler, the days were a little shorter. Jack would never make it to Christiana's wedding.

The initial resentment Jack received from Marbry when he held steadfast that the children and he "should not and could not accompanying her for her weeklong mid-September trip for her sister's second wedding" seemed to dissolve. Jack insisted that taking the children out of school and having him travel away from work would not do anybody good. Marguerite came down to sit for the kids and things seemed to be peaceful all the way around. Marbry almost delighted in the freedom that "being back in Montreal solo would bring." Several uneventful months flew by, with Jack embracing his new sales position and Marbry meeting more frequently with her "book clubs." Twice a week she would "travel to Renton for a new book club."

Sitting down one late spring evening in the wicker chair on the east porch, Jack moved an array of Marbry's novels to the side. Falling out of Marbry's copy of Scott Smith's *A Simple Plan* was the itemized MCI phone bill separate from the actual bill, which lay on Jack's desk with all the others to be paid.

In all good probability, Jack would have never noticed the itemized portion if it had not leaped out at him. There were a litany of calls to a "212" number. Even calls to Trent's number wouldn't have seemed out of the ordinary if it weren't for Marbry's paralyzing defensive reaction when Jack brought the attention to the expense of the calls.

"Who do you think you are to question me about my calls to my uncle?"

"I'm just bringing attention to the expense…maybe your INVESTMENT COUNSELOR can call you on his dime."

The following Tuesday, the office of one of Jack's important clients in Seattle called Jack en route to a sales call to cancel the buyer's appointment, as he "had caught the flu."

Looking at the bright side, Jack thought, "A little extra time with the fam," as he headed back up North I-5 for an early afternoon.

Walking up the stairs to his house, Jack felt his attention unnaturally fixed on a nail squinting through the steps. An unsettling breeze blew off the bay. Opening the door, he could only wonder where Marbry was. Picking up the mail, Jack found the usual array of bills, junk mail, a postcard from Tom from Tijuana signed "Tom & RB." It looked like things were going well for the two, as now they were on vacation and it was nearly three years they were together, their music crisp, the sounds of their story, a synchronicity of love.

Nearly masked underneath that giant-sized postcard was an envelope with highlighted red markings circling it from ARCS Mortgage Company stating "Foreclosure Sale information."

Slicing his right index finger from ripping the piece of mail so hurriedly, Jack could only stare at the ominous foreign words and message that this piece of mail was stating. After reading the words "Mr. McKenna, the foreclosed property at..." Jack could feel his heart pounding through his buttoned dress shirt.

The name was correct.

The address was correct.

How could this be?

Immediately calling the 800 number, Jack angrily described the "terrible and defamatory letter he'd received in the mail."

The customer-service operator calmly repeated back, "Sir, that house has been in foreclosure since April."

Jack could feel the back of his shirt starting to saturate with sweat. Odd, since the temperature was merely fifty-five degrees.

"That's impossible," Jack responded. "I personally have written, signed, and mailed the check every month."

"Sir, I can get you my supervisor!"

Minutes waged on.

A friendly but gravelly voice finally came back on.

"Mr. McKenna?"

"Yes."

"First off, I want to inform you that our conversation is being recorded, do you understand this, and do you approve of this recorded conversation?"

"Yes...yes."

"As Miss Gregor informed you, we have had that house, and I'll repeat the address..."

"Yes, that is the address."

"As I was saying, we have had that house, Customer #19934567, in foreclosure for seven months."

Jack, exasperated, pleaded, "Sir, I have sent in those monthly payments every month."

"We see that, but there has been a stop payment on each and every one, each and every month. Since the timing in our system allows them to be cashed, our computerized system automatically cuts a check that has been sent out...let's see...to you each month...Mr. McKenna, could you hold?"

Jack waited.

"Mr. McKenna, is the information sufficient that we have provided you?"

"You were saying that a check has been sent out to me by your system?"

"Yes."

"Well then, do you in fact have my endorsed signature on those returned checks?"

"Mr. McKenna, I am going to forward you to our legal department."

"Mr. McKenna, this is Mr. Harper from the ARCS Legal Department. What can I help you with?"

"I don't know where to start...I'm shocked by all of this...I will contact my attorney, of course, but I would like to agree to fix this if this in fact is really happening."

"Mr. McKenna, this is already happening, there is a lien on that house. I suggest you have your attorney contact us immediately."

Jack telephoned his attorney, Carl Rosen. Rosen was another connection from his hockey days, as he was one of the well-established sports lawyers in a firm that had offices in Toronto and Vancouver. Rosen negotiated acquisitions and representations of both teams and players in his heyday, but moved to Bellingham to settle in as "a country lawyer." Rosen was able to get Washington Mutual and its mortgage carrier, ARCS, to have the delinquent mortgage placed in forbearance. With interest and fees, Jack owed twenty thousand U.S. dollars.

His next call was to Cooper. Always receptive to conversations with Jack, Cooper again immediately took his call.

"Cooper is there anything else I need to know about Marbry?"

Jack explained what seemed like a scheme to Cooper. It appeared Marbry had been receiving the checks and endorsing them, and they were going into some account other than their mutual account, or any account Jack was privy to.

"Jack, I'll do anything to help, but now is the time you must follow that money...Morgan could not have done this by herself."

"Following the money" meant only one thing to Jack...Trent.

Shattered Glass

Jack CONSUMED HIMSELF WITH GETTING everything and everyone he could to help himself out of this mess. When he called Arne back East, Arne immediately offered, "Well, we can rule out any aiding and abetting from your idiot brother-in-law, that guy Monroe."

Jack, staying serious, said, "Absolutely agreed on that."

"Jack, not to be Captain Obvious, but that guy is the master of the malapropisms… I'll never forget at your wedding when he asked Bennett where the laboratories were, because he had too much to drink… Bennett didn't catch it first that he was looking for the lavatories. I chimed in, 'I'm with ya…my sediments indeed'…Jack, I'm sorry, but I'm trying to bring light to this very pathetic situation you're in."

Arne had the right type, but the wrong time.

"Arne, I really appreciate the gallows humor, but that was Chester; this brother-in-law is even dumber!" Humor wasn't what he was looking for when he called Arne, but after all, as Arne put it, "That's what friends are for…to get you through difficult times whatever way possible." Arne offered to float a loan, among other suggestions, so Jack wouldn't have to borrow with high interest. Jack told him while he appreciated it, he was giving himself twenty-four hours to figure everything out, and part of that was speaking to Marbry.

"Jack…can I be woefully honest with you, and say some things that may be painful for you to hear?"

"Of course."

"I respect what you want to do…but as far as I see it, you have two major things to deal with, and, Jack, I mean deal with, without blinders…one, come to the realization that Marbry isn't who we thought she was, and two, understand the word extortion doesn't just mean getting money by threat or force… it also means to gain illegally by ingenuity…I'm convinced, and have been for a long time…the bizarre checking activity…the missing ATM money of yours, etc., was going all to one place… your so-called investments managed by that reprobate Trent Doertz…didn't Cooper so much as tell you?"

"Well, like everything else surrounding this mess, his message was cryptic…but he did seem like he knew his family was up to something nefarious, and I should watch out."

"You need to stay close to him."

Jack would soon find out Cooper was closer to him than he thought.

Marbry finally came home, and she was with Agnes-Marie.

"Jack…can't believe it…what are you doing home so early… how was the meeting?"

Able to stay calm enough to pick up and hug Agnes-Marie, Jack responded as best as he could. "Fine."

Looking concerned, Marbry said, "Jack, everything okay?"

"Aggie, can you go upstairs? I just want to talk to Mommy."

The sky was overcast, but there was a sliver of sun peeking through the windows as Jack sat down and asked Marbry to do the same.

Benn burst in, leaving his books on the cluttered kitchen table, announcing, "Who's going to drive me to soccer practice?"

"Benn, I will," Jack answered. "Just give your mother and me a few minutes to talk."

Benn, turning away toward the kitchen door, said, "Oh, what about, boring adult stuff like mortgages and stuff?"

"Yes, Benn, exactly."

By now Marbry wore the frightened look she'd had the night at the Horseshoe Café when Jack spilled the beans about his knowledge of her deviancy at Lowenthals'.

Jack couldn't wait any longer.

"Where are we, where are we, where are we supposed to live now, Marbry?"

"Jack, what in God's name are you talking about?"

Taking the updated foreclosure notice and ARCS envelope off the top china shelf where he had left them, Jack threw them on the table.

"Why, how, could you do this...you created it, and worse, you hid it...what kind of person does this to her family?"

Shouting back with a face of violence he had never seen from this woman, his wife, Marbry screamed, "What kind of person takes me out to a foreign land like this, because HE loves it?"

"This is paradise next to Montreal! It's so bad that you couldn't ever discuss this? You just steal my money, or rather extort it!"

"It's OUR money!"

"It's all my hard-earned money, and this was my hard-earned home."

"Everything is yours, Jack, or so you think...your dreams, your job, your place, your house, and I've had it."

Picking up the empty kitchen chair, Jack threw it westward, shattering the bay window into mega pieces.

Standing by the door, Agnes-Marie was sobbing, "Please don't hurt us, Daddy."

Marbry took this opportunity to grab Agnes-Marie, thrusting her out of the doorway, saying, "I'm leaving…"

She shouted at Benn, who stood at the top of the stairs, "Get in the car, and get in now."

Benn, his demeanor calm despite the adults' augmented anger he and his sister were witnessing, said forcefully, "No, Mom, Dad's driving me to soccer practice."

Marbry and Agnes-Marie would stay with her friend Lucille that night. Jack, after Benn's soccer practice, would enjoy a revealing hamburger and dinner at Fiamma's with Benn.

Explosion

JACK WAS SIMULTANEOUSLY SURPRISED AND dismayed at Benn's indifference to his mother's return. Escorting him to his bus stop, Jack told Benn, "Mom will be back later with Aggie after I fix some adult things." Benn, crossing the street, gave his father a penetrating, inscrutable stare, waving unforgettably.

Jack returned to the house, and so did a bottle of Jack Daniels along with him. He knew he had to take care of this disaster immediately. Calls to Lucille's house were unanswered, and a little bit later a Federal Express truck pulled up in front of Jack's house. Jack could only think, "Oh no, another paper document with a notification of negligence." The return address was Calgary, and inside was a stark white envelope. Inside the envelope, a yellow sticky paper read, "One thousand apologies on behalf of my family—Cooper." It was attached to a cashier's check in the amount of twenty thousand U.S. dollars.

Jack sprang from his chair, calling Cooper right away.

"Cooper, I can't accept this."

"Oh, Jack, but you must."

"But why, Cooper, from you...you don't have anything to do with this."

"Jack, I do."

Cooper continued in earnest, "Jack, the last time we spoke I told you I needed to speak with you at Christiana's wedding."

"Honestly, I don't remember the words 'needed to,' Coop."

"Jack, please, we are all complicit in this...I wanted to tell you what Trent did to that Monique woman among others...I felt all along that Morgan was funneling funds to Trent that weren't hers...I wanted to tell you, but I felt you were so blindly in love with her...and the romantic in me felt like perhaps you COULD work it out."

Cooper continued in a regretful tone, "I wished so much that you were at the wedding so I could speak with you face to face, give you a wake-up call in person. When I witnessed how much time Morgan was spending with Trent, I knew he had manipulated her, like he had so many people...Jack, you know this is UGLY stuff, you must accept these funds...consider it just payment for what my family has done to you...please accept this. You, I'm afraid, are going to have to deal with perhaps a lot worse, my beautiful man."

After thanking Cooper, Jack drove downtown to deposit the check in his bank, and wired funds immediately to California, erasing the forbearance, and the foreclosure. Doing so, Jack cringed at the perverse feeling draping his body, understanding the treacherous web he was ensconced in.

Whether the bottle emptied out of relief or of the realization of a love and dream dead, Jack Daniels sufficed as Jack's lunch that day. Marbry finally called, but it was not a mediating ring. Hysterically screaming into the phone, Marbry ripped out words describing how Agnes-Marie was playing in Lucille's backyard with Jenny, her daughter. The house was in sight of the Whatcom Creek on the north side of town. Shortly after the bus dropped them home from school, the girls, playing in the backyard, came running in, screaming, "Mommy, Mommy, the river is on fire."

A gasoline pipeline operated by the Olympic Pipeline Company had ruptured under Whatcom Falls Park. The Bellingham Fire Department had the neighborhood evacuated, but now, an hour and a half later, the girls were still shaking.

Jack, wavering from thinking he never should have drank to knowing he had to get to Marbry and Agnes-Marie, placed his head under the kitchen sink in a valiant attempt to sober up. Jumping into his car and heading up to the fire department, he stared into a plume that seemed apocalyptic as cars pulled off the side of the road as if Armageddon had hit. Running into the firehouse with sweat down his back, he embraced Agnes-Marie. As he hugged Marbry she could only cry, "Look at what you have done to us in this God-forsaken place."

The Inevitable

BY NOW THE DIE HAD been cast. The idealist, the romantic, had run almost head first into the tree of reality. No matter how many leaves of color dropped in front of him, Jack had been still convinced it was the summer of his life. Peering out the window on this part of his life, Jack noticed with suddenness the trees were all bare.

Jack went back on the road for sales calls Thursday. The anonymity of calling on customers who were not part of your daily routine, who did not see you week to week, watch your moods, know your personal life, made it easy to hide any sense of personal turmoil, any sense of personal loss. Perhaps, Jack thought, in a momentary reflection of self-honesty, this was why the sales life was appealing. Other than the conversational display of the kids' cute pictures, and the anecdotal exchange of their lives, customers, clients, people could never really know you. Anecdotes were the lifeline of a salesman's pitch.

Jack knew deep down life was not an anecdote.

The divorce papers arrived Friday. Marbry, still conveniently at Lucille's, called to make sure Jack "received his copy"…and told him that she would be back in the afternoon to pick up Benn. Jack didn't bother responding. Staring at the papers, he could only read that his marriage, his previous dozen years, his life's outlook, even his dreams, had now been wrapped and packaged under the title "Irreconcilable differences." The words on a document had now created this alien within him that he did not recognize. The dishes had piled up in the kitchen sink the last couple of days, as he had no appetite for cleaning, and Benn's cereal boxes were strewn across the kitchen table. The regret of choice now released a rage-induced scene of broken pieces of china all over the kitchen. Cornflakes and puddles of milk laced the floor the way his affection for Marbry had, cold, barren, spoiled.

For the first time in his life, Jack felt the cloak of loneliness draped around his shoulders like a dusty blanket kept in the attic for too long. He drove himself down to the Waterfront bar. It was barely late morning, Lynne had been in setting up, and as Jack settled in at the bar, she cast her caring brown eyes upon him. "Jack, surprised to see you here at this time?"

Jack, looking up, responded, "Lynne, hi, just one boilermaker."

Lynne stared for several seconds, a near refusal stare, eventually bringing over the drink. A millisecond later, the drink was gone. Jack ordered another. Lynne took the time to grab his glass, saying, "Jack, this isn't going to solve your problems."

Jack looked up at her, realizing here she stood, an angel, and the weighted cloak of loneliness was, at least for now, lifted. Leaving a twenty-dollar bill on the gleaming wood bar surface, Jack, getting himself up and peering at Lynne, softly muttered, "Thanks."

Loneliness and rage can often leave a person just as fast as they come. A matter of seconds after the temporary reprieve he had received from the angelic bartendress, Jack's cell phone rang. It was Danny.

"Jacky Boy, you got a complimentary call about your 'follow-through' from Cusky Sports Empire, but where the hell is last week's field report?"

"Putting it in the mail this afternoon, Danny, end-of-the-school-year stuff has just delayed me a little bit."

"No worries, Jack, Portland has been pleased with your numbers…listen, we've got the box for Saturday's Mariners game, if you want to invite your family and your three best customers…it's twelve tickets available…"

"Thanks, Danny… I'll get back to you."

Later that afternoon Jack got back to the house. Marbry was there alone. She had signed Agnes-Marie up for dance lessons and Benn was not yet home from school.

"You here to clean up that disgusting mess in the kitchen?" Marbry said with bitter authority.

"Yes, and I'm here to relax at home with my kids."

"Well, I'm taking them away this weekend."

"Not without me you're not!"

"Jack, get used to the idea that you will need my permission to see them."

"Marbry, what has happened?" Mustering a laugh, Jack calmly said, "You seemed content over the years, you never kicked me out of the bed, what was it…the magnetic allure of your uncle Trent? Just give me something, right here, face to face?"

With a demonic look in her eyes that Jack had only witnessed a squint of once before, Marbry shouted back, "This has nothing to do with Trent…this has to do with us, and mainly YOU. Read the divorce papers…this is a D-I-V-O-R-C-E. I'm not speaking anymore…just have Benn ready to go by five."

"Marbry, no can do…Benn isn't going anywhere."

"Are you crazy, Jack, don't you get it? I would have to be a drug dealer or a prostitute doing it in front of the kids for you to get custody of them."

"I think you're horribly mistaken on that...but good luck, have a nice weekend," Jack answered, now with bitter authority.

Deceit

A QUICK, IMPORTANT CALL TO Carl Rosen relieved Jack that Marbry, at this point, would have no exclusive rights to take the children away. The kids would come with him to the Mariners game and they would be surrounded by friends. Jack invited Tom and RB and Davis and his family and his three favorite accounts. Davis brought along his recently divorced sister, Betty. Betty had sadness written in the theatre of her face. Ever the big-hearted brother and friend, Davis whispered to Jack, "She's very depressed, I thought it good to get her out, with folks like us, Jack." The Mariners would be playing the first-place New York Yankees.

Driving down to the brand-new Safeco Field, Jack regaled the kids with stories of how the Yankees were "the second-most successful sports franchise in history." He of course would ask, "Who is the most successful sports franchise?"

"The Canadiens," Agnes-Marie and Benn would scream out simultaneously.

It was a joyful day. Agnes-Marie toyed with RB's red bandana and playfully RB tied it around her. Agnes-Marie wouldn't know the baseball score from Adam, but she loved the attention from this woman, now a renowned rock star and a cool human being to boot. Not having shaved for a few days, Jack had a pronounced stubble, which prompted Danny to call him "Black Jack McK."

Tom was playing at the Crocodile Café next weekend and demanded Jack come to their concert. The "Blasters'" platinum album was discussed more that day in the box than the score of the game. A side conversation was brewing after the sixth inning, however, as it was noticed that Jack had several hard cocktails. Jack had always had a reputation for being an alcohol prude, so his increased imbibing didn't go unnoticed, particularly by Tom or Danny.

"Hey, what's going on, what happened to our old two-beer Jacky…I remember when you were the designated driver before there was a designated driver!" Danny announced in good humor.

In the eighth inning, Agnes-Marie left the secure arms of RB, inquiring to her father, "Is somebody going to drive us home?"

Quickly realizing the complexity of Jack's chosen afternoon activity, Tom astutely reached out. "Jack, we want you guys to stay over at our new place in West Seattle, the kids will love the place…the front yard stares out on Vashon!"

Tom, having been provided a cursory tale of Jack's current woe, suggested he call Marbry, even inviting her down. Tom knew the weapon that would be used if Marbry even sensed Jack's slurred speech. It was a good strategy, as Marbry, as charming as kittens in a courtyard to Tom when he called her, gave full instructions to be given to Jack, allowing them to stay overnight.

The overnight stay in West Seattle, the ferry ride to and from Vashon, the bike ride around the bucolic island, Agnes-Marie and Benn splashing each other in the frigid waters of the Puget Sound, and the marshmallow roast outside of Tom and RB's house were enough to have Jack forget the turmoil that had recently been, and that he knew was coming in greater fashion. For as brilliant as the sunset was that blissful night overlooking

Vashon, he felt a sense of dread that transcended the arrival of the divorce documents.

When the kids went to bed, Tom and Jack got to talk.

"Jack, the kids look great…you look like shit."

"Thanks, Tom…I'm guessing you know I feel like utter shit."

"I don't want to sound like your rabbi, but you can't booze this crap away…you've got to deal with it and speak to someone. This is wild, but you'll never guess who came to one of our gigs… never in a million years would you guess…"

"I don't who…Pierre Trudeau…?"

"Close…Tony Edmonds…Ed…Father Ed…Remember him?"

"Wait a minute, 'Call me Ed'…the Wellingtons' priest friend?'

"Yes… he's out here now at a parish in Seattle. You know, he's a guy you might want to speak with. Before he became a priest, he was very much into music, and he actually worked for Key Bank. He's loved in this city…and very accessible. The word out there is there's somebody you know who you would never believe speaking to him about some pretty heavy things…but I'm NOT going to invade his privacy and I'm NOT going to be the one to shock you with that," Tom stated laughingly. "Jack, I think he would be a great person on many levels for you to speak with."

"C'mon, Tom, I could always call the Rev. Billy Graham."

"Seriously, Jack, we are all upset at what's going on, we know it really sucks for you…just trying to help."

"I know, but what is he going to fix, my broken marriage? …I can't figure out what happened…it's just like a meteor came and crashed into our lives… Thanks, Tom, but my head is still spinning."

"Jack, know we're here for you…we want to be able to help in any way…not for nothing, but I saw some things coming. You know there's been this what I call 'vibe' going on in Seattle the past few years. It's really why all the great music is coming out of here... I'm no psychologist but I believe this is why something special is happening here, even if it's just music. There's a lot of different people creating a lot of different sounds...but there's just this great VIBE, everybody is into everybody else's energy. Honestly, I never got that vibe around Marbry and the Wellingtons...they have so much...but it seems they're just moping around their mansion of misery in Montreal... Jack, we want to dedicate a song for you...we just hate to see a joyful being like you caught in a depression!"

"That's pretty corny for you guys...doesn't that go against the genre of alternative rock?"

"Jack, NO, that's just what it's all about...we sing about reality, real shit...that's why people relate to this scene now... Jack, we met these guys who were from Western up in Bellingham... their lyrics are pure poetry, and they are masterful musicians... they are going to be big...there are so many people down here writing, singing, coping... It would have been good for you to keep that guitar... We were so pissed that Marbry sent it back... that night when you told us that, Rachel said prophetically, 'I'm so sad because she's robbing him of any music in his soul.' Well, that was the very least that she robbed."

"Tom, I'm fucking angry...I really am."

"Jack, that's why you've got to speak to someone."

By midweek, with Marbry sleeping in the outer room of the house, and Jack still in his bedroom, Jack woke from a night of no sleep to a knock on his front door. There stood an affable-looking stranger apologetically asking for "Jack McKenna."

"That would be me."

The young man announced, "I am serving you 'A Modification' to your Divorce of Affidavit of Service that requests you to appear before the court." As Jack read them, the words elaborated exaggerated details of "Mr. McKenna's excessive drinking in front of the children." The second-to-last paragraph called for "Ms. Morgan McKenna to receive FULL CUSTODY of Agnes-Marie McKenna and Bennett McKenna." It further outlined the "absence of an appropriate domicile for the children." Jack, adhering to the request of Cooper that "Marbry or any member of my family need not know of the check," never had informed Marbry that he had received outside help, from inside the family, to get the house out of foreclosure. Marbry had maliciously and safely assumed that the house was still in foreclosure. She would of course have known all too well that Jack's funds were too limited to save himself or his family from this unforeseen calamity. Or so she thought.

The next day, Carl Rosen called.

"Jack, I suppose you are retaining me, as I received some calls and paperwork from your wife's attorney."

"It seems like they have everything figured out. I didn't even know I was going to retain you as counsel, but that's fine with me. You are the only attorney I know or trust."

"Well, they seemed to have shored up some ammunition, and looks like this was a long time coming, I'm afraid, Jack."

"It seems quite apparent that way, Carl, but I'd better come into your office, as this crap is overwhelming me."

"From what I can see here, I can understand why."

Jack met with Carl the very next day. Carl's office was a comfortable barrister's office...not ostentatious like the stuff of movie legends, but more real. Cedar-paneled walls, framed family pictures, and the golden gavel he'd received from the Bar Association for his "outstanding tenure of integrity" in his county-court judgeship earlier in his career. Jack stood staring at that as Carl walked in.

"Pretty impressive honor…why did you leave that for private practice, Carl?"

"I got tired of fighting the tawdry battles of politics and law…now I'm just fighting the good fight in the tawdry battles of law, period. Jack, sit down. Who's this Betty Hughson Daigle, anyway?"

"Betty Hughson Daigle, that's our former neighbor and friend Davis's sister, why?"

"Well, she has a bug up her ass for you, my friend."

"How so?"

Carl proceeded to throw a document across the table. It was a signed affidavit stating how the witness "observed excessive drinking in front of minors at baseball game and barbecue."

Jack could only shrug. "Wow! Guilty as charged for the ball game, but the barbecue, the worst thing I did there was scream when Agnes-Marie pulled my chest hair when I was trying to get her to come out to me in the pool."

"Well, credible or not…it doesn't hold up well, especially with this other stuff in the complaint."

"What other stuff?"

"Your alleged flirtations with one Rachel Beliveau."

"RB? …Wait, really…that's Tommy's partner, lady…this is not nuts… it's comical."

"Yeah, the way it reads here is that you took the baby and traveled to Canada with her and another man…"

"Oh my gosh…Carl, I'm going to get sick, seriously… She was working…"

Cutting Jack off, Carl said, "Like I said, welcome to the tawdry world of law, and in this case, the tawdrier world of divorce."

"Why is she doing this…I thought we just had 'irreconcilable differences'?"

"Jack, do you need to know what she wants or what she doesn't want?"

"Well, I sure as hell know what she doesn't want, but what does she want?"

"She wants the kids and Montreal."

"What about the house? I'm sure she wants that as well."

"No, Jack, and funny thing, technically it would be easier for her to get the children if she had the house, but she clearly doesn't want to be in Bellingham, and it seems like a concession of sorts."

"That's because she doesn't even know I got the house out of foreclosure… They're just being coy. Carl, she can have everything, she can take the house, sell it, she can take my freaking hockey sticks and underwear, but she's not getting my kids. Carl, I can't begin to tell you how I feel the last decade of my life has been stripped from me…but she's not keeping me from the kids' lives."

"Jack, let's talk tomorrow and I'll speak with her attorneys. By the way, your brother-in-law Cooper called, and he wants to know if he can help you with anything?"

"Cooper?" Jack felt oxygen come in the room in the midst of a stifling, bizarre morning.

Double Standard

GETTING IN A CAR AND traveling to a client became now a catharsis in the midst of the turbulent tornado of his personal life. The anecdotal relationships with his customers were now ones to be cherished. Jack loved the industry and loved the customers that existed in it. That affinity was mutual, as Jack was invited to his customers' weddings, bar mitzvahs, and christenings. The raw energy of the socialization of his vast client base enabled Jack to usurp the upheaval that at times he would deny the very existence of.

But it did exist.

Arne was coming out next week to meet with clients of his own in Seattle, and he wanted to get together with Jack.

Enjoying lunch with one of his better customers in Tacoma, Jack was brought smack into the aroma of reality through a call by Carl Rosen.

"Jack, your ex and her attorney called and are digging in their heels...they are going to fight for full custody."

"Okay, so be it...let's fight..."

"Jack, I'm going to need copies of your last ten years' worth of salary statements, bank accounts, and checking accounts for discovery."

"I'll get it all."

"What do you need from me, Jack?"

"Carl, just your continued good counsel and friendship."

Jack was convinced, from what Benn had told him at their burger dinner together, that no judge would release a child to what, according to Benn's own words, were pictures of instability of his own mother, whom he loved very much.

"I hate when that guy calls Mom."

"When does that happen?"

"Dad...too much when you are at work...and she always lowers her voice, takes the phone upstairs, and is in a bad mood when she gets off the phone. Ask Aggie...one time she went upstairs and told Mom to get off the phone, she needed help with her homework, and Mom spanked her...Aggie was really upset. If it's Uncle Trent, you know his own kids hate him."

"Why do you say that?"

"They tell us whenever we see them in Montreal...they can't believe you play with us and talk with us...they never see their own father, and they never want to see him...the guy's bad news, I know it's Mom's uncle and all, but nobody likes that guy...he's mean."

"Well, we don't need to talk about him...I want to hear about your soccer."

Jack knew full well custody of the children would mean their living in Montreal, and the unreal world of the Wellingtons.

In the few years prior, which now seemed like a millennium ago, when Jack first announced that he was leaving hockey, Uncle Mac's malaprop of an A.E. Housman quote laid a sting in him for quite a while. Before realizing how poetic he could be, Mac blurted, "Your athletic career was, as Housman said, 'a garter briefer than a girl's.'" Jack laughed to himself, understanding the Freudian slip, but the truth of the message was valid.

Gnawing at him was the perpetual question, "did he leave the game too soon?" That choice was, of course, his. Now his marital romance had withered seemingly briefer than the garland he thought he wore. Jack knew he would "die young" if he had to be separated from his children.

Within this family that swallowed him in and spit him out in the vomit of their virulence, there existed a palliative antidote in the flesh and blood. That was, of course, Cooper. He needed to speak with him, first to work out a payment plan to pay him back, and then to hear his words that were always grounded in care and concern.

"Cooper, I need to know how I can arrange to pay you back."

"Jack, again, consider this indemnity for the protection you unwittingly never thought you needed. Jack, I know you all too well to not know what you're calling about."

"I'm sure you do, Cooper. I have accepted something terrible now in my life, but I just can't accept a separation from my children."

"I know that, Jack...but if it's any consolation...even if it means spending more time back with my troubled family in Montreal, I will do whatever I can to make sure those children are reminded about the love you have for them."

"Cooper...I think it's you who are the beautiful man...I need to ask you this...Cooper, do you have...I mean I think I can ask you this now...do you have...?"

Cutting Jack and his anxiety off, Cooper answered, "Yes, Jack, I do have a special someone, and so you can imagine the suffering I have to live with in my very own family."

"He was never accepted?"

"No…I don't have to tell you, the parade of Trent's harem was all fine and dandy…but I am the black sheep, as I told you a way long time ago!"

"Coop, I'm ashamed, but before I got to know you, before all this, I thought…well…"

Cutting Jack off again, Cooper said "Jack I know you're a prolific reader, so you would know Herman Hesse…he said whatever good or bad fortune comes our way, we can always give it meaning and transform it into something of value."

"I believe that. That's why it feels like we're soulmates, Cooper."

"Now you get it…because we both know and understand what love is."

Driveway Depression

THE SONG WAS NOW A hit. The Blasters introduced "Driveway Depressions" at the Crocodile Café to the swoons of a crowd ranging from their faux-ID twenties to the Botox-intoxicated, graying, flat-chested women in their fifties. The raspy voice of RB roared through the microphone, lifting lyrics that were suddenly overnight the anthem of the disenfranchised divorcées.

Heartaches trembling
He lives in the past—
She wants the green
lane of life so fast
He cherishes her tunnel of love—
she thinks orgasms surrender
only to diamond-studded gloves.

They got themselves a driveway, driveway, driveway depression.
Driveway, driveway depression.

Everything looked so neat
tidy and suburban—
He a bit country
She channeling Cosmo
riding on Urban.

Trying so hard
yet
not seeing her path—
He wants love
should have looked further
She's full of wrath.
He looking to mediate
some sort of confession
She wants pearls, a pool, and a sunroom extension

They got themselves a driveway, driveway, driveway, depression.
Driveway, driveway depression.

Can't they see…kids one, two
He thought almost three—
She wanted no more
shocked was he
Seeing her flying out the door

There's only a driveway, driveway, driveway depression
Talkin' a driveway, driveway depression.

Carl called back with the "settlement offer" from Marbry, her attorney, and the Wellingtons. Hearing, and ultimately seeing, the offer, Jack realized this whole ordeal was nothing short of Manichaean. Marbry's attorney stated that "Ms. Morgan was willing to part with children Agnes-Marie McKenna and Bennett Walter McKenna for the holidays of Easter, National Patriot's Day, Canada Day, Labour Day, Thanksgiving Day, alternate Christmas vacations, and summer vacation in exchange for their full custodial presence throughout the remaining days of the year. In addition, the sum of thirty-eight thousand dollars will be returned to Mr. Jack McKenna." Grasping his gut, Jack listened to Carl's words of attempted comfort.

"Jack, we can fight this because what's clear from this to any judge is that Marbry doesn't want any part of the children... she wants them all the days that they will be in school and the nannies will be nurturing them...that's what I see...don't you see—you're going to get them when they are most available to be with you—summer, holidays...Jack, this is great."

"Is it? It all sucks to me."

"Yes...I know...but what they could have tried to do... I'll fight this, Jack, if you want to..."

"Carl...what's the thirty-eight thousand total from?"

"Oh yeah, that's the number that Marbry acknowledges 'borrowing from your accounts,' does that sound right?"

"Carl...it could be more, it could be less...it's, it's..." Jack's voice fell off.

"Jack, listen, if you can present evidence it's more, we'll..."

"We'll do nothing...I'll fight for the kids but to have this thing reduced to a dollar number..."

"Jack, I know...this is tough...whatever way you want to go with this...go ahead, let me know... Don't you have that mediating session tomorrow with the court-appointed child psychologist and the kids?"

"Yes. And honestly it will be the first time I will be face to face with Marbry since this whole thing has unraveled...now that her sister has gotten her a condo in Seattle."

There were calls waiting from Bill, Arne, Tom, Davis, Rachel, Marguerite, and one from Danny on his answering machine. Jack couldn't bring himself to speak to anyone that night. They were messages of kindness and compassion, even Danny's, which surprised Jack, since, in a self-realizing moment, he admitted to himself that his productivity was off.

Jack would be bringing the children from Bellingham to Everett for the session. Pulling off I-5, Jack caught a cursory look at the logjam amass on the Snohomish River. The lumber lay still, seemingly in a spiteful manner underneath the smooth stratocumulus puffs that were so out of reach.

Her sister, who of course, like always, stood in the hallway always welcoming, always shining, always there at the most hideous of moments, drove up Marbry. A reprieve from spending any more unsolicited time with the unabashed agent provocateur was had when a Nurse Ratched-looking woman opened the door of the doctor's office, stating strongly, "McKenna family only." Christiana would have to momentarily suffer alone with her innate schadenfreude outside the office.

With the doctor still tied up with another patient, Nurse Ratched notified the family, ever ironically, "to make yourselves at home," seemingly twisting the knife. Benn chose to stand in the north corner away from everyone. Jack sat down on the east end of the long couch, with Marbry on the opposite side. Agnes-Marie placed herself firmly with arms folded right in the center of the couch. Looking to her mother at her left and her father at her right, she stretched her ten-year-old arms in such a way that it seemed they each took on an extra foot. Her left arm was on her mother, her right arm on her father. The delicate arms, now taking on a life of their own, found their way around each of her parents' necks, as she pulled them with all her little girl's strength to the middle. Jack never felt so sad in his life.

Nadir

It HAD BEEN A LONG time since Jack had been able to speak to or get together with Bill Bensen. Although the conversation centered on minor-league hockey tidbits of the Spokane Chief's quest for the Memorial Cup, and how strong a fight the Portland Winterhawks were going to give them dominated their call, there was much more Bill wanted to say. First and foremost, he needed to convey his concern to Jack and how bad he felt "he couldn't be with his buddy during this trying time."

"Jack, I've had a handle on everything from Arne, but man, shit…I'm so sorry for this."

"Never saw this coming, Bill."

It was the long pregnant pause after he said that that grabbed Jack in the throat. Jack felt Bill's honest response coming like a tornado over a prairie.

"Jack, I have to tell you, at one point or another we saw this coming."

"I don't know if I should say how so?"

"You don't need to, Jack; you did all the right stuff. You loved, man, that's what you're supposed to do…bad things sometimes happen to good people…"

"Thanks, Bill, but I feel the worst is coming."

"Jack...no, no, no...man, don't make it worse...you're going to tell me that there is going to be a fight for the kids, right...and that's going to be ugly?"

"Well, yeah."

"Listen to me, brother...this is the only thing I can offer... those kids love you...nothing is going to ruin that...everything I've heard about that family, they are going to come at you with their lawyers and their money...that's what they got...that's not what you got...but you have a lot more...a lot more...and I'm not going to go and tell you what you got...but nobody is going to take that away...man...don't drag yourself, your kids, and your family through that shit..."

Jack told him of Agnes-Marie's hug and pull at the psychologist's office... In a way he was reaffirming what he felt, what Bill was telling him.

"Jack, you are going to have to suffer a little for a lot later... but holy fuck, you are a hockey dude...you are a stud...you will get through this...you know that...don't make it worse...I don't know martial arts, but you have to take their negative shit and absorb it and stay with your good karma...it will work out in the end...and you'll have your kids and a loving family one day... trust me."

A long time ago in a hockey galaxy far away, there was this kid who loved to play the game, and he turned his back on that game. The teammates, the friends, the brotherhood that emanated from that game never turned their back on him. Jack knew this all too well, now more than ever. Stephen Crane's words in "The Open Boat," "It would be difficult to describe the subtle brotherhood of men that was established here on the high seas," came alive in the depths of Jack's cranium. For he would now experience high seas of his own, but pulling the oars alongside him would be those sacred friends, and he was going to need them now more than ever.

A day later Carl Rosen called.

"Jack, the Wellington lawyer called up and he emphasized they are going to St. Bart's for ten days, but when they get back they expect an answer to their offer...I got to tell you, and I'm keeping this lawyer-to-client private, but these are the most entitled sons of bitches that have come down the pike in my experience. Jack, we of course are going to trial! ...Jack? Jack, you still there...?"

"Carl, yes, I'm here. I'll take the offer...she gets the children for the days she wants, and..."

"Jack, you sure you know what you're saying...we CAN do better, Jack, you sure...you're owed so much...I think we can get you full custody."

"Carl, love you, man, and everything you have done for me...but it will all work out in the end...my kids love me, and I love them."

Carl knew all too well this was not the conciliatory voice of a reasonable man; this was a conciliatory voice of a broken man.

Twists

WHILE JACK FELT THINGS CRASHING down on him, things were starting to unravel in the staid, proper world of the Wellingtons of Montreal. The sordid way they lived their lives could often go unnoticed. That would only be believed by people who bought into the myth, the charade, the Wellington masquerade. Up until now the worst fate to fall upon the clan visible to the public was the botched Botox of Millicent. At least that was a known "terrible fate."

There had been another the year before, when Kendra Picard, one of Trent's previous romantic interests, filed a sexual-harassment suit against Walter, which apparently took place a decade before when "Mr. Wellington forced himself upon her in the Pearl Guest Room," according to papers filed in the Magistrates Court. That "unfortunate incident," as described by Millicent in her deposition statement, disappeared as fast as it was mentioned. This was remedied by Kendra's loss of memory about details, and her dropping the charges. While few were ever close to the Wellingtons, those who were whispered to the press a hush; that "hush" was money— apparently $250,000 in "hush money."

Shock and awe came to the family when Trent Doertz went down. Trent had spent the better part of his past three decades weaving and winding through the manipulations of people who came in contact with him, only to stand as the "willow" of the Wellington clan. Trent once famously bragged while talking shop at a family gathering, "In a firm of three partners, it's always two that stand together, making the decisions, wielding the power." Whether it was that fact that was indeed true, or he misunderstood the machinations of the angry third man out in that partnership, there was one partner of the three who brought Trent's house of cards down.

Bill Carey, the not-so-silent partner of "Reynolds, Carey, and Doertz," supplied both the FBI and the SEC ample evidence of Doertz's bilking of apparently two hundred and forty clients through Doertz's elaborate plan of "cherry-picking." Carey first became aware of this one still summer day when he was literally accosted by the normally genteel Harrison LaPointe, a fellow member of the Montreal Hunt & Game Club. LaPointe grabbed Carey by the throat, turning it the shade of Carey's flipped-collared pink Lacoste polo shirt.

"You guys want to make money…fine…but to rip my mother's savings away…you will pay for this."

Heather Bettencourt LaPointe, Harrison's mother, often referred to as "the doyenne of the club," and, in some circles, the "Matriarch of old Montreal society in the nineties," was a ninety-year-old still with her wits strongly intact. Harrison LaPointe rehashed an encounter his mother had recently had with Trent Doertz at the office in New York.

Mrs. LaPointe had entrusted her estate in the hands of Trent Doertz. She had known him as a young boy at the Montreal Hunt & Game Club, the son of one of her bridge-playing friends, Penelope "Poey" Doertz. She wrote him a recommendation for Cornell University and actually bought one of his Chryslers for one of her servants when he was selling them out of the States. Although the car lasted less than three months, she was quite impressed when he showed up for the wake and funeral of her husband, Baxter. A few days after the funeral, he wrote her a beautiful sympathy card, telling her how "Mr. LaPointe was like the father he never had." Naturally, when he came to Mrs. LaPointe a month later, informing her of his new investment career, she felt she just couldn't refuse this "kind and considerate young man." She would have no reason to believe her investments weren't at the very least monitored and well-stewarded by this "polite, handsome, and distinguished-looking man she felt she knew quite well."

Requesting an update on her portfolio, the wily Mrs. LaPointe contacted R., C., & D. Taking more than adequate time to supply her with these updates, the firm seemed in disarray. Heather understood something didn't seem "kosher" to her. Perhaps it was the vagueness of the office manager, Cathy, or the previous lapse in the rudimentary paper statements, which were no longer coming in the mail.

Two days later Heather and her daughter, Elaine, flew to New York for a previously promised "shopping excursion" they had planned. Her real intention was to confront Mr. Doertz, her "personal broker."

With the appointment scheduled for 2:00, Doertz kept her waiting for two hours, something not normally experienced by the well-regarded Mrs. LaPointe. When she finally was given the opportunity to meet with him, there appeared to be something tawdrier about this man than she could have previously imagined.

"Mrs. LaPointe, so good to see you. I would love for you to come to the club out east my wife and I belong to. My apologies for keeping you waiting, but with such a bull market, I had to watch the transactions, I mean trades, until the close of the market, you understand."

"Not really, Mr. Doertz. I appreciate the tea and Brie you have provided for me all afternoon, but this 'bull market' you have alluded to hasn't really been so bullish with my account, not to mention I am indignant about the fact that as an advisory client there has been little or no communication as to the status of my account."

"Mrs. LaPointe, Heather, if I may, it hasn't long been a bull market, you know. Please, you are like my mother, you remind me of her, and I would only treat you and your account the way I would treat my mother, my sister…"

Cutting off the rambling Doertz, Mrs. LaPointe told him, "I want full disclosure of every transaction regarding my account in the next month…"

"Mrs. Lapointe, you are not fully understanding the nature of this complex business."

Listening to Doertz attempt to explain the significant lost margins in a bull market, she stormed out of the office knowing she had been, as she told her son that night, "fleeced by an American wolf in sheep's clothing."

Not aware of Mrs. Lapointe's encounter with Doertz, it took several minutes for Carey to realize what Harrison LaPointe was even talking about, or so he claimed later in his immunity deal with the government.

However, it wasn't long before Wallace Reynolds, the founder of the firm, and Carey, along with LaPointe and one third of the victims of Trent Doertz's scheme, were sitting in a boardroom alongside government attorneys. Pleading innocence, Reynolds and Carey were granted immunity for full cooperation in the SEC's case against Doertz. What they didn't know was that the SEC case two years before had gone up in smoke when the government fumbled the original allegations of cherry-picking ignited by Monique Lavillière. Although the exact negation of Lavillière's testimony were never fully known, Doertz's attorney, the corpulent Brent Cassiday, lawyered well enough to have her portrayed as a "spurned lover of Doertz reaching for straws to discredit a man of distinction." Still, the FBI had continued to watch the firm for the past two years.

But now, with several prominent victims and two partners willing and able to testify, the government had a substantial case. The government's case looked ominous. "Cherry-picking" was a violation of the Sarbanes-Oxley Act. Doertz had a masterful plan of buying blocks of stocks and waiting until the end of the day to see if the trades were profitable. If they were, they would be assigned to a hedge fund firm called Stratospheric Horizons. If the trades were not profitable, they would be assigned to one of his clients' discretionary accounts, the likes of Heather Bettencourt LaPointe's. "The damages amounted to over three point five million dollars to investors," according to Arne, who followed the case from beginning to end, and seemed titillated by the sheer "hubris of it all," or so he told Jack.

"Arne, just why, especially at a time like this, does this start and dominate your phone conversation…the only thing different now is that it appears that there is an official proclamation that this guy is a douchebag?"

"Jack…more like an official proclamation that he is a criminal! But more importantly Jack, don't you get it…don't you see any connection here to your victimization?"

"Arne…you lost me. What connection?"

"Jack …you know I really like your attorney, Carl, but I don't understand why both you and he readily accepted the settlement of thirty-eight thousand. The sheer number of that 'settlement' shouted out to me that there was something more going on there."

"How so, Arne?"

"Jack, I know your memory can be muddled right now, but all those missing funds and mysterious checking accounts, and the cash stolen out of the Lowenthals' till—WHAT DID SHE DO WITH ALL THAT MONEY? Unless she had a drug habit, or something of that sort…where did that money go?"

Jack was in a daze; he really couldn't hear the words Arne was saying to him. While money, lost money, was certainly a part of the betrayal he felt, it was an insignificant part of it all. It would be tantamount to trying to convey to a Canadian hockey player that his career-ending injury was going to cost him X amount of dollars. The most debilitating aspect of that injury to the player would not be the loss of money the injury brought on, but the loss of his passion, his love, his ability to play the game. To Jack, this was more than a career-ending injury, this was his love, this was his life, this was his family; the money loss was just a slight muscle tear in the soleus.

The demons were now parking in the recesses of Jack's mind. It was another Friday afternoon and he was driving alone through downtown Seattle, on the heels of an unaccomplished sales day. Was it his loss of self, a depression, or the seemingly unsellable white skating boots?

"Jack, are you trying to sell us hockey boots or female figure skates?" one retailer told Jack jokingly.

The only substantial sale of the week was a one-thousand-piece hockey-stick order to sports giant America's Maple Leaf Enterprises, better known as AMLE.

"I could use the resiliency in my body that the carbon fiber in theses sticks offers."

Jack was speaking in self-effacing earnestness, and that was what "sold the sticks," the buyer told him, signing the order sheet. Escorting Jack out of his office, Trey McCallum, the owner and buyer, set his eyes on Jack's stomach, commenting, "Jack, if you're drinking that much beer, let us in on it!"

Drinking now had become Jack's catharsis, and it became visually apparent that he was doing his fair share of it. This afternoon would be one of those fair-share days.

The waterfront streets settled into the gloaming as the foghorns from the ferries created a feeling of emptiness, of things happening far off, of voices longed for, far away, in the booming distance. Those voices of course were the voices of Benn and Agnes-Marie. They swirled in the cacophony of the corner of his mind as he swirled another black-and-tan at Mulleady's Pub. When a young family came to dine, the laughter, the conviviality of family, created a bleeding, or so it felt, in his intestinal wall. While he thought he was soothing that wound, drinking was burying his reality. Jack was starting to lose more than just his reality.

To his right, a portly man in a wrinkled suit, looking as worn as Jack felt, struck up a conversation with him. The two hit it off as he bragged about his season tickets for the Mariners games. The fellow was kind enough to insist on buying rounds for whoever was in earshot of him. Jack attempted to turn the conversation toward hockey, in which his newfound friend, Don, had little or no interest.

"I'm an American sports guy…not a hockey guy." The happy ignoramus continued, "If it's all right by you, I'm not good with remembering names, so I'll just call you 'Hockey.'"

As long as "Don" was buying the beers, Jack was not even considering taking issue with either of those two strange, oafish comments.

"Did you eat yet, friend?" Don bellowed.

"I had enough bar food during happy hour for the weekend," Jack replied.

"Well, I think it's high time you and I take a ride up 99 to Muffins."

"Nah…not interested in any more food."

"Food…I take it you've never been to Muffins?"

"Can't say I have."

"It's a nudie joint—can't drink, but you won't want to once you see this assemblage of tits and ass."

"Nah…maybe another time."

"C'mon, you look like you could use more than your share of tits and ass…where's your car?"

"In a parking garage."

"Perfect—you seem like you started drinking a lot sooner than I did…I'll drive."

Whatever compelled Jack to head up and out with a guy whom he'd known for the lesser part of forty-five minutes to a world he knew even less defined the strait he found himself in. The seediness of the corridor that led into the place was only compounded by the cast of characters who were both customers and dancers.

"I feel like we are on a set of a movie of a Damon Runyon novel…"

"Damon who...oh, I take it he was some hockey player..." the baffled Don retorted.

"Yeah...something like that."

"C'mon, Hockey, let's get lucky."

While the woman looked just as lethal and poisonous as the men, Jack found himself in conversation with one pleasantly plump blonde identifying herself as "Daisy." She seemed to be a little bit wiser than Jack figured for someone to be stationed in this den of sleaze.

"How did you get into this?"

"You talk to me this long, you owe me a few dances, Sweet-Eyes."

Bringing Jack to a room several feet away from the stage, she put out her hand. "One hundred for a half hour with Washington's finest, you got the pearl of the place, Sweet-Eyes."

Jack broke out in laughter; her mention of "the pearl," in this over-lit room adorned in a pink-petaled façade, could only invoke in his mind Millicent's Pearl Guest Room, another room where sleaze and sin overtook the four walls.

Sticking the Ben Franklin adroitly "where the sun don't shine," Daisy commented, "I don't know what you're laughing at, but I'm going to make you cry with pleasure in a few heartbeats, Sweet-Eyes."

She didn't let down on her promise. "Daisy" tossed and turned her robust fleshiness clad in nothing but a yellow-flowered G-string...Jack marveled at how she moved...agile in her plumpness, tender in her gyrations, focused in her attempt to please. Thirty minutes of this was more movement, any kind of blood-circulating movement, than he'd had in quite a while.

When the thirty minutes were up, Daisy went from rapturous lover to stern businesswoman.

"Sweet-Eyes…I gave you my best—now reach into your pocket and give me your best tip as a sign of respect."

Another hundred bucks gone…and with his new friend Don nowhere to be found, Jack had the better sense to get out of there and somehow find a way to call a cab. Leaving, Jack sensed someone following him. Still without anything on resembling clothes, Daisy, with a look of a concern, whispered seductively, "I'm here Fridays, Sundays, and Wednesdays…why don't you come by…you seem different than most." Jack nodded; it had been a long time before any female force gave him a sense of affection, no matter how real or unreal it was.

Jack was fully alert, thanks to nine cups of Coca-Cola in the past two hours, and he tried to clarify to himself where he just had been to, what he had just done, what it all meant. For now, he convinced himself it meant absolutely nothing. Jack was fresh in the fringe of life, a life he understood to be a different one, but paradoxically the same. There never seemed to be any preparation for what was around the corner for him. There was no rehearsal, no practice. As Ken Dryden put it in his book, *The Game,* that every real hockey player or fan read as "the bible" of the sport, "…that's the American way. Canadians played, Americans practiced." When he was back in the Canadian Juniors, it was game after game, the idea being experience honed you, made you better. He gave up a life he'd practiced the whole of his young life to enter an unprepared life with the likes of Marbry and the Wellingtons. Here again he was meeting up with life as it was given to him, and he was playing to the best of his ability. He never really seemed to stop, other than for a brief minute, and question where he was going. He took the joy, the sadness, the suffering, the pleasure, and embraced it with whatever skills or knowledge he had or didn't have from experience or the lack of it. Going through life that way, as he had for the past decade, was not the surest route to joy and fulfillment.

Monday morning, Jack was getting himself ready for two afternoon appointments in the Tacoma area. The phone rang and it was Danny McDevitt.

"Jack…rough few weeks, eh?"

McDevitt's tone was loaded, and Jack spun his answer to describe his health.

"A little bit of a cold, but other than that—I'm feeling pretty solid."

"Jack…the numbers don't seem so solid…you have fallen well off in all adult skate categories."

Stunned by McDevitt's immediate assertiveness, Jack tried to stay positive. Speaking about his stick order with AMLE, his youth sales numbers, and his appointments that afternoon, Jack found himself forcibly self-promoting.

"Speaking of youth, Jack, I have to tell you—corporate has had some expectations of you, considering your background, to bring the inner-city skate program along in Seattle."

Jack could or would never call in the "crutch" to what was existing in his personal life, but he knew McDevitt knew, and it seemed that he was bombarding him strongly with negatives.

"Danny, I have copied you on all my paperwork regarding my proposals with all the necessary city agencies. Jerry shared with us even in Atlanta where it went so well, even there it was a considerable process."

"I realize that…but do what you can…WE all need to really push. Let's meet down in Seattle a week from next Wednesday."

The little window of hope Jack received from Dan was when he stated the "WE" in "WE all need to really push." While it was the most aggressive conversation he had ever had from Danny, Jack knew full well it wasn't his personal problems, it wasn't his loneliness, it wasn't his undiminished drive.

He was sure it wasn't him. It was the market. He knew that from keeping close to all his fellow reps around the country. Jack kept close to them by phone on a regular basis, in an effort not to commiserate about a slowing market, but to figure out along with his teammates "out in the trenches" how they could strengthen their sales. No one player could ever win a hockey game, and Jack knew that, and no one rep could regain a marketplace. Thus, Jack created a "let's do it through ideas and communications" network with his fellow reps. One of his fellow reps in the Midwest called him "our captain." But despite that can-do attitude of Jack and his sales colleagues, and the marketing might of Nike behind them, the sales reps found their own insurmountable adversaries in the pricing of the product, the diminishing interest in the game in the States, and the notion that "in-line skating" would be the next big recreational sport with resultant sales. It was falling in the very streets it was well-anticipated to take off in.

The next week was not more productive, and certainly not hopeful. Wednesday came, and Jack was at Elliot's on the waterfront in Seattle for a scheduled lunch with Danny. With a sense of foreboding, Jack arrived an hour early for his noon luncheon. With the bar opened at eleven, he could start fortifying himself with some "Jack and Di" specials. Uncharacteristically a half hour late, Danny turned the corner to the bar part of the restaurant with a three-piece suit on, file in hand, with another equally overdressed-looking corporate type alongside him.

It couldn't have been five minutes before the words from Danny came out: "Jack, we're going in another direction." Danny was speaking while his corporate mate for the day stared blankly. Jack didn't remember a thing spoken after that.

Jack had felt for quite a while that he was an ember in a fire that, once ablaze in a vigorous, glowing ferocity, now was turning wildly destructive. He'd felt that about the company ever since Nick Manatee, the Southern California rep, had put it that way. Manatee, one of the most successful manufacturer's sales reps in the business, drove a red 911 Porsche with the license plate "Igot#s." That was merely a window into his magic as a salesman. In the business, they would say, "Manatee could sell a fly off street shit."

Manatee's salesmanship made companies. Manufacturers would often send their marketing people to shadow him in his various territorial marketplaces. His horn-rimmed glasses and his vintage checkered blazers gave him a panache that was uniquely his own. He exuded confidence. He was the master of the presentation of the product and the close of the always-successful sale. Jack remembered McDevitt telling him, "Had Manatee been born several hours to the north, that confidence of his would have made him an incredible threat as a hockey player."

Performing was Manatee's game. What intrigued his fellow reps about him was that he swore he was never on the road "after 3:30." As if it were a magical time, he explained that was "board-room time." "Board-room time" meant, of course, to the well-informed, time on his surfboard. Manatee, riding the image of a smooth playboy, was really a meticulous worker who understood the balancing act of intense preparation and detail, combined with a fit lifestyle. Manatee believed a salesman was most productive when he or she had a goal beyond the numbers at the end of every day. Manatee's daily personal goal was to ride the longest pipeline every afternoon. His path to production often clashed with image-conscious corporate bean-counter types. When one of the company's regional sales managers, Tom Bendix, came to travel with him early in the year, Bendix insisted he set an evening appointment.

"For what reason?" Manatee inquired to the anal-retentive Bendix.

"So we at the company know you are working a full day."

"Well, that's just stupid, isn't it about producing? My numbers speak for themselves," Manatee replied.

"Yes, but just like an updated file system that needs to be looked at every day, our salesmen need to be in the field every day from sunup to dinner-time…it's an important part of the image we want to show our stockholders."

Manatee answered directly, "You need to shove that lack of logic back to Oregon."

Bendix wrote him up. In turn, Manatee requested to the sales V.P., "Please don't ever let that luddite back in my territory."

Two weeks later Bendix was let go.

Manatee had a pulse on the market like no one else. He had told Jack a year earlier, "If in-line skating isn't going to happen in my territory, it's not going to happen…I'm holding on to my other sales lines." Manatee could be prescient in his words.

"Just remember this, Jack, I know you're this loyal Canadian ex-hockey dude and all, but loyalty doesn't stretch out in this industry…sad to say, but there's no reciprocation of loyalty in this world. Companies come and go, and before they go, it's always the salesmen that go first. You want to give your left nut to your company, don't. Work hard, but remember most of these companies have no soul."

Those were certainly words to remember, but Jack was feeling his soul was already being ripped out by uncontrollable forces. Walking up to Pike's Place Market, he strolled by the Pure Food Fish Market. It seemed to him like it was just the other day he was bringing home fish for Marbry and life seemed so right, so real, so good. Walking down back toward the waterfront, Jack soon was in the warmth of a crowded Irish pub. It was Wednesday, he recollected, and after a few scotches he'd hail a cab and head up to Muffins. He'd stay an hour, get the attention he craved, convincing himself he would figure out where he was going.

"Sweet-Eyes, you're back…don't tell me you're back to talk?!"

Already three sheets to the wind, Jack replied, "Only for Washington's finest!"

"I don't know if you're going to feel anything, Sweet-Eyes, you look like Sad-Eyes tonight."

"I can't even begin."

He didn't. Jack was seeing pink, feeling dizzy—and then he was out. Next thing, he was waking up in a sun-drenched dayroom with daisies plastered across the wallpaper. Getting up, he couldn't help but start to vomit, finding his way to a minuscule bathroom. Daisy was at the door.

"How did I get here? Where's my wallet?"

"You can thank me for getting you here, and here's your wallet, minus a few dollars."

"Whaaat?"

"Listen, you were out before you even saw my lap. It took me a lot of money to get help to get you out to my car…you can thank your lucky stars…don't worry, your credit cards are all intact, and hey, guess what…you'll have to trust me…you're lucky something told me I could trust you…but you can stay here and get your shit together, I have to get to work."

"Work…what's going on…aren't you—"

"Yes…I'm all that to supplement my income, but I teach management classes at the community college, and I have a ten o'clock class."

"I suppose you teach Bible school as well."

"Not yet, smart-ass…but for a guy who—"

"Okay, listen, Daisy…can we…is that your real name?"

"Call me Sophie during the day."

"Okay, Sophie, I have to get back to Bellingham…but my car is in Seattle."

"Sweet-Eyes, Jack, you'll have to figure that out."

"Can we, can we get together…? This is all so unreal!"

"It's so unreal, and lucky for you, but again, you wouldn't be here if I didn't want you to be."

"Daisy, I—I mean, Sophie, thanks."

Back in Bellingham, Jack had much figuring out to do. Arne was the first one he called. "Jack, there's something going on, isn't there… I haven't heard from you in quite a while."

Arne for once was silent when Jack let him in on the details of his firing. But he wasn't about to pull any punches when he started to let him in on the "Daisy story."

"Jack…man, I'm here for you…but don't go down that road."

"Just what road is that?"

"Jack, I know things have not exactly been rosy for you—but we're talking about a stripper here—a veritable whore."

Arne could only hear the din of the phone smashing on the receiver. Lara quickly asked Arne what had just happened.

"Pretty much my most stable of friends has lost his wife, his job, and his mind." Being the friend he was, Arne wasn't about to let his friend continue to "piss his life away." Calling Jack's cousin Tom, he filled him in, commenting, "Tom…Jack's life right now is darker than your songs."

Jack had to wrestle with his lost job, his lost family, his lost self. As if that were not enough, at 10:00, he received a call from a man identifying himself as "Detective Jim Flaherty of the Seattle Police Department Fraud and Identity Theft Squad."

"How can I help you?" Jack asked curiously.

"Well, we can help you. Immediately you need to cancel all your credit cards and notify your bank about what has transpired."

"Let me ask you, Detective, why would, of all people, a detective from a fraud squad be calling me on a landline?"

"I understand your concern, but we are working on this with the Bellingham Police Department, so I am going to recommend you go over there immediately after we speak…and…"

"What exactly is going on here?"

"Let me cut right to the chase, Mr. McKenna. You have been the subject of an ongoing investigation over the past few years, but now we understand you are the unwitting victim."

"What?"

"Your incident at Muffins is part of a much-larger fraud, and my calling you is a result of a successful sting we did there with an international ID-fraud ring."

"You knew I was at that place…I think I should call my lawyer."

"Again, Mr. McKenna, from our end, we now understand you to be a victim here, and immediately, your ID has been stolen, and fortunately for you, you can clean it up right away."

"The part of my being a part of an ongoing investigation over the past few years, what is that about?"

"Mr. McKenna, I can assure you, you are safe, and what just transpired was a separate situation, but at your convenience, I would like to meet with you in the coming week. You can have anybody you trust present, but it's best we speak in person.

"One last thing—Daisy…she's not Daisy, she's not Allie, she's not Sophie—her real name is Sandra Mortana. You got drugged, my friend, and while all your cards were left intact, her crew scanned every number on every card in your wallet. The real scam is leaving your cards physically intact so you suspect nothing wrong. Had our sting not been successful, you would be paying bills for somebody identified as Jack McKenna in India or Germany or Russia."

Jack did exactly as the detective told him, and he called Arne, hat in hand.

"I think I owe you an apology…sorry for being a dick last week."

"Jack, you weren't a dick, you just let your dick govern your reasoning. Well, Jackie...the Wellington folk must be mourning in Montreal."

"How so, what now?"

"Well, the sentencing that the judge handed down at Trent Doertz's trial a while ago, eight years, was held up in New York."

"I bet the family didn't expect that!"

"No, neither did he...and he only made it worse for himself from day one."

"Let me guess...he exuded arrogance."

"Jack, it was like arrogance on steroids. During the trial he readily invoked the fifth...apparently he never disclosed to the clients that the firm was engaged in the 'cherry-picking.' His attorney's defense expert claimed that 'there was no loss to the clients, just a gain to the favored accounts.' To add to the salient smugness already displayed to the government, his attorney requested a Fatico."

"What is that?"

"It's what that judge back in the nineties in the Michael Milken trial gave Milken...it's basically a hearing where the judge reviews allegations disputed by the defense to help determine his sentencing...you wouldn't remember this probably but Milken cooperated with the prosecution, and the prosecutors even agreed to the reduced sentence. But as I said a long time ago, Trent Doertz is no Michael Milken. Old Uncle Trent was dismissive from start to finish."

"No surprise there."

"My buddy at the SEC told me that Doertz made himself the poster boy of arrogance and greed, starting with the Maybach sedan he was chauffeured in every day to court."

"Well, he couldn't have come in a used Chrysler...he sold them all in Canada."

"Very GOOD, Jack...but just reading the accounts of the trial in the *Journal,* you could tell he made himself a marked man with the government. In his lawyer's appeal they made him out to be strapped financially, that this would 'place an undue hardship on the family,' and that he is at risk of losing his house in the palatial Hamptons."

"Oh, he could always fall back on the mercy of Millicent."

"Oh, trust me, he did...she was one of his victims."

"Get out of here—"

"No, I'm serious—both she and her best friend, Celeste, were among the victims."

"Wow, sonuvabitch...no holds barred, this guy."

"Jack, you could almost read the government prosecutors playing the miniature violin for him. The greatest line from the government was that 'the defendant should not receive special consideration because he lives in a three-million-dollar house in the Hamptons rather than a housing project in Harlem.' The judge, famous down here, Lorraine Quinn, in her summary said Doertz 'abused his trust' and that he—Jack, are you ready for this—had a penchant for dishonesty."

"Well, he had a penchant for a lot of things, and certainly dishonesty was among them."

"Jack, what do you hear from Marbry?"

"Well, not so much, other than the arrangements for the holiday visitations with the kids, but I wanted to ask and tell you something."

"Shoot, Jack."

"Arne, you were always so inquisitive about Marbry and that whole weird financial stuff, the missing money, the bounced checks, the foreclosure—what were you trying to piece together?"

"Jack, wouldn't it seem a natural connection, considering all of that weird stuff and Marbry's odd relationship with her uncle Trent, that she was somehow involved with this, or maybe even something seedier...I mean, Jack, we all had to walk on eggshells wondering that and trying to ask you that...we knew how you felt about her."

"Trust me, Arne, those feelings were watered down quite some time ago. I actually think the most nefarious of all of them was her sister Christiana...somehow I feel Uncle Trenty boy was not as clever as all this and Christiana was..."

Before Jack could finish, Arne jumped in, "Jack, yahoo, finally you got your head out of the sand.

"The next time you visit the kids we want to be up there with you. I've got to go now but Lara wants to see you and the kids and I want to speak to you about some Nike stock." There wasn't enough time for Jack to start telling Arne what had developed before he was off the phone. Seemingly before he was even off the receiver with Arne, Cooper was on the phone.

"Jack...Jack, have you been called yet?"

Jack didn't even recognize the caller at first. The usual voice of calm that defined Cooper was melted in a harrowing echo of fright.

"Cooper...are you all right."

"No...Jack...you don't know do you!?" "They said they are going to wait twenty-four hours before calling you..."

"COOPER, what is going on?"

"Oh, Jack, it's Benn, he didn't go to school, he didn't come home last night, nobody knows where he is."

His neck tightening, his stomach swirling with atomic waves, Jack shouted, "No…no…I must get back there…oh no, Coop, please tell me…"

"Jack, the SPVM have been notified and I believe the RCMPs are involved…Jack, I am so sorry…but I must tell you…I don't believe it's a kidnap or something…Benn has been so sad-looking of late. The children, Jack, oh heavens, they are so distraught without you…I think he's just depressed and he's running away from all that…"

"Cooper, all what?"

"Jack, my family seems more closed down than ever…it's bad."

"Cooper I'm getting a flight out of Vancouver…after I call Marbry."

"Jack, yes, of course you must call Morgan, but, Jack—reach out to Helene…I'll just say this—she's been your children's savior through all this."

Jack had to subdue his anger before he called. After all, why would he not hear from Benn's mother first? His thoughts immediately ran to what would Benn do, where could he be, as he dialed Marbry.

Jack could get by Marbry's almost too-calm tone, but it was her detracting answer to his question as to why she didn't call him immediately that surged a choking lump in his throat.

"Why didn't you call me immediately, Marbry?"

"Oh, come on, Jack…you know how you are…you would get over-emotional," Marbry answered ever so smugly.

"How is Agnes-Marie?"

"She's fine. She's not the one missing."

Jack valiantly controlled his response.

"Are the police with you now?"

"Of course not. They are where they are supposed to be—looking for our son," Marbry answered in a chillingly somber tone.

"Marbry, have you been given a sedative? You seem overly calm."

"No, Jack, I just don't see any point of overreacting to this or anything the way you are known to do."

"Well, I'm coming out."

"If you think that's going to bring back Benn, well, fine then."

That last comment by Marbry made Jack fully realize that she was no longer just the long-lost woman he'd once loved in a marriage that fell into the grips of an opulent but dysfunctional family's pull. The palpable pull that existed in the notion that she had gotten herself involved with someone "well beneath her station in life," as Millicent once put it. No, he now saw Marbry herself as an embodiment of evil, of treachery, of lethargy. This demonic presence was not healthy for his children. He questioned now how Marbry could have any sense of love and nurturing for the children.

As he rushed out of the house to drive up to the airport, the phone rang but again. Jack decided not to answer it. He had to get on a plane and get to Montreal to be there when Benn was found. Turning the key to lock the door, he heard the phone ring and ring, soon stopping. With the door locked, he reached down to pick up his bag. The ringing started again. Jack thought, "Perhaps it is the police with news." Unlocking the door and rushing to pick up the phone, he heard someone on the other end, breathing heavily, but not speaking. Jack knew who it was.

"Benn, you all right, where are you?"

Sobbing in measured bursts, Benn answered, "Dad, we want to be with you."

"Benn, I want to be with you—can I come to where you are?"

"Yes, Dad, I am at the Greyhound bus station."

"Which one, Benn?"

"In Vancouver, Dad, Vancouver… I was lonely like you were, Dad, but I went to the station to get to you."

"Benn, I'm coming right now to be with you, but I have to call the police so they know you are safe, and they will probably pick you up."

"Dad, just promise me you will be with me right away."

"Benn, I'm going to set speed records to get to you."

Jack immediately called the police in both Vancouver and Montreal, Cooper, and Benn's mother Marbry, in that order.

Jack was impressed with the concern and professionalism of both the Montreal and Vancouver police departments. They immediately dispatched officers to the bus station and instructed Jack to meet up at the Salish St. station. A large bespectacled man by the name of Sgt. Gordie Eagleson introduced himself to Jack and brought him to the room where Benn was devouring hot chocolate and hot food. Hugging interminably, both Benn and Jack cried and cried. Through streams of tears, Benn kept saying, "Please don't leave us, Dad, please don't leave us."

Cooper had contacted all members of the family Jack did not have time to, and Marguerite and a wobbly Uncle Mac soon arrived at the police station, all adding to the hugging. Jack was interviewed by the detectives and the youth bureau representative separately and then together with Benn.

A social worker came in and put Marbry on the phone with Benn. Jack could not make out what Marbry was saying on the other side of the phone, but the brevity of her conversation with Benn was chilling.

The social worker pulled Jack aside and informed him that "permission" was granted by the boy's mother through an interview in Montreal for him to stay temporarily with his father. This consent was needed, as "a fifteen-year-old boy needs his mother, provided she is alive and willing." The social worker also explained that he was "not allowed, however, to leave the country."

It was agreed that Benn would be staying at Marguerite's home for the time being until all was figured out. Jack and Benn spoke for hours back at his childhood home after an incredible meal fixed by Marguerite. At about ten o'clock Benn passed out on the couch, and didn't move an eyelid when Jack picked him up and carried the one-hundred-fifty-five-pounder into Jack and Preston's old bedroom. Jack had let Benn do all the talking, but what stood out to Jack was Benn's descriptions of how "Mom's never around…she's always going somewhere with Aunt Christiana…thank God Aunt Helene is always taking care of us." Recalling how Cooper had so much as advised him to reach out to Helene, Jack knew now he had to.

Jack called to thank Cooper for everything, and he reluctantly requested Helene's phone number. Cooper seemed like he had it memorized, adding, "Jack, this is good." There was no question; Cooper always did know and care about what "was good."

Jack had often thought about Helene over the years, the warmth of her voice, the sheer honesty within her reflected through the beauty of her deep caramel-colored eyes, her strong sense of maternal concern for her children, yet he felt oddly guilty about those thoughts. Though she was long-divorced from her repulsive ex-husband, Trent, Jack felt she was still all too close to a family that was now becoming more of a nightmarish part of not just his past, but his present. Yet, now it seemed right to call her, and though 9:00 p.m. here, it was midnight in Montreal.

"Jack, Jack McKenna, I'm so relieved that Benn is safe and sound with you." The soothing serenity of her voice negated any feelings of awkwardness Jack had felt about reaching out to her out of the blue. It was now close to dawn in Montreal and Jack was saying goodbye to Helene, forgetting totally it was nearly 3:00 a.m. where he was.

It was surreal to be back home with Marguerite and Uncle Mac. Among the chaos of finding Benn, Jack had much to tell them. Preston, who had finished law school and was now practicing in Massachusetts, called offering advice on where Jack could go from there with any custodial pursuits.

"I appreciate the offer, Preston, but Carl Rosen has been with me through my mess, and I wouldn't want to burden you with this despair."

"Jack, any way I can help, please let me know… I love you and those kids."

The expression of affection from his older brother was something Jack had never heard, and he intimated that to his mother, Marguerite.

"Jack, you two were always night and day, but he always loved you and was proud of you. Not having any kids of his own, he really took to Benn and Agnes-Marie. I'm sure Marbry told you about the times he came to Montreal when you couldn't and took them to the museums and parks."

"No, Mom, she never did…I never knew."

Marguerite, never one to editorialize about another's relationship, calmly said, "She had so much going for her… couples have problems, but we couldn't believe how she changed toward even us. Anyway, the main thing now is to know that Agnes-Marie is safe."

"Mom, she is, she's with Helene Lemieux."

"How do you know this?"

"I spoke to her last night…for quite a long time."

Glistening through her gray but still very alert maternal countenance, Marguerite answered, "I get a sense you're blessed with her being there."

"Almost providential intervention, it appears, Mom."

"Jack, for the time being, let me spend a few hours with Benn…he's been talking about how much he needs skates, and you know I know where and what to get him. Mac really wants to speak with you…you know he's slowed since his fall last year, but nothing has slowed in that brain of his."

"That would be great, Mom."

It was again too long since Jack had spent time with Mac, but his voice was always important. It was the voice not only of experience but from another world. Again Jack could only believe it was in part the voice of his father beyond the grave.

"Jack, I can only tell you one thing…I get too philosophical when we get together, but I need to tell you this, and this only."

"Mac, you know I always take to heart whatever you tell me."

"Well, not really, Jack, but …"

The two men broke off in laughter.

"Jack, as I told you that beautiful day in Stanley Park after Bennett's death, I am very proud of you, always have been. Now, I know it's hard to believe that I have never forgiven you for leaving hockey, or moving to the States when we know Canadians live longer, are better educated, have fewer divorces…" Mac's voice started to trail off. "Jack…let me get to the point. Jack, I feel like a failure; I needed to be firmer with you that you needed to stick with your dream… Hell, it was a noble one. Trying to use sport to change broken kids' lives for the better. Hey, remember that time you called me when you first moved to Bellingham, and you had hiked on top of that mountain…what's it called, Chainsaw or something…"

"Chuckanut."

"That's right, Jack, I remembered it well because of what you said and how passionately you put it. You said—do you remember this, Jack?—you said, 'Mac, it's beautiful here, I see these forested islands in the distance, and although they are far away like my dreams, I'm going after them and I'm going to pitch my tent on them.'"

"Yeah, I remember something like that."

"You had to get off the phone because in the background people were laughing, and you broke your profound thought of intensity."

"Yeah, that was Marbry and her sister when she was visiting."

"Jack, think of it…this is hard to me to say, but the only time you ever had problems was when you diverted from your dreams. Dammit, I apologize if I didn't let you know how important it is to stick with your dreams, even if they conflict with whoever or whatever in your life laughs at them."

"Mac, I get that now, probably a little too late."

"NO, JACK, NO, it's never too late to follow a dream. Now, you have a lot of shit to get in order, but remember what I'm telling you, and I'm not lecturing you, you know that…never say never to your dream."

"Thanks, Mac, I needed to hear that."

"Jack, it's never too late to focus on change in your life… It's time I let you in on my new change."

Puzzled, Jack remarked, "Change, Mac—what change would you be taking on at this point in your life…don't tell me you're getting married?"

"Jack, to me, right now, something better…a conversion."

"A conversion…whaaat?"

"Jack, I don't know if you remember that fellow, the priest, who was at your wedding?"

It was all coming back to Jack.

"Father Ed? Eddie."

"Yes, I never told you, but we had a long talk back then, and we keep in touch regularly."

Shocked, Jack didn't know if he was putting him on or what. "Mac, with all due respect, you're the original Catholic bigot."

"Yes, we all have our demons… Forgiveness is an important ingredient to our existence…I blamed the Catholics, the Catholic faith, everything Catholic for something that went wrong for me, oh, too long ago. I just didn't want to go to my grave with this hardness of heart I've been carrying…and I realized, how could I hate them? So many of the people that have helped me, funny thing, they were Catholics who didn't scream it out—they just believed in something: Angus, his brother, Father MacDonald, Ed…"

"Uncle Mac, I don't know what to say."

"I have to tell you, Jack, I have preached to you a lot in your life, but this might be the most important thing I'm going to tell you. Father Ed invited me to this speech about forgiveness by this New York City policeman who was shot in the line of duty and relegated to a wheelchair, paralyzed for life… Weeks, days, after he was shot, with a beautiful wife with child, he forgave the attacker, and for the better part of almost three decades, he's traveled worldwide and inspired millions to embrace forgiveness—the guy got to me. It's a crazy thing, Jack—his name was MacDonald Stephen—no, no relations to the priest who was so good to you in Connecticut. Things haven't gone so great for you, Jack, but first and foremost, you are going to have to forgive, even if you can't understand this life crap, and the next thing, you're going to have to embrace something spiritually of purpose; I'm not telling you what religion—that's a personal choice—but you HAVE to embrace the spiritual world the way you embraced hockey long ago and so many things you gave your best to, no matter what cards you were dealt."

Contemplating wholeheartedly everything Mac threw at him, Jack could only muster, "Thanks for being in my life, Mac."

His weathered skin now aglow, Mac shouted back, "Now get back to that Chucawhatever Mountain, and get the important things together!"

Pragmatics

THERE WAS SOMETHING THAT TRANSCENDED all the personal needs that Jack had to deal with. He knew he had to sell the house in Bellingham. While his severance package from Nike was fair and equitable, he was determined to gain immediate employment. But now, first and foremost was a man-to-man conversation with Benn. Judging from their conversation the other night at the bus station, it was not going to be easy. And it was not.

"Benn, we need to have an important talk."

"Dad, before you start, I'm not going back to Montreal... except to help you pick up Agnes-Marie...besides, she's with Aunt Helene and she's been more of our mother."

"While that may be true, she's not, and your mother is your mother."

"Dad...you always told me to honor her and all...but the simple fact is she's never around."

Jack knew he couldn't and shouldn't negate what Benn was saying, but he needed to get him to face reality. After all, the jurisdiction of the courts was in favor, and would be always in favor, of a mother's custodial rights first and foremost. But certainly, Benn wasn't making this up, and what he was describing amounted to abandonment.

"Benn, we have to figure this out, and as soon as your mother calls, we all need to work this out."

As he waited for that call, Jack's cell rang with a "206" number. It was the detective from Seattle, Jim Flaherty.

"Mr. McKenna, I was wondering if tomorrow was good to meet with you in Bellingham."

"Detective, I would like to, but I'm in Vancouver for a few days."

"Well, it would be really helpful if we met; there has been some movement in the case I alluded to."

"Movement, case…I'm not sure we spoke about a case."

"Well, I did mention the investigation…it concerns you and your family."

Confused, Jack let the detective in on what had transpired with Benn's running away.

"Mr. McKenna, when I show you what I have to show you, you might even understand your son's motives more completely."

Hearing that, Jack didn't hesitate to say, "How early can we meet down there, Mr. Flaherty?"

"I'll be there by 9:00 a.m."

"So, will I," Jack answered firmly.

The expected call came from Marbry. What came from the dialogue was not expected. Gone from Marbry's tone was the contentiousness from the conversations of the recent past.

"Jack, I hope you are doing okay through all this."

"Marbry, I hope that as well for you… How's Agnes-Marie?"

"Good, I spoke with her tonight…she's still at Helene's… she—they—are quite fond of Helene…she wants to be with Benn in the worst way and Jack…Jack…"

Marbry's voice broke off in what sounded like someone trying to climb a mountain and speak at the same time.

It was a voice moored in melancholy that he hadn't heard since her explanation of her uncle's "suffering." "Jack...I can't do this...I can't anymore."

"Marbry, what can't you do?"

"Jack, they want to be—to be—" she slowly repeated, "with you...I've failed."

Staggered by Marbry's comments, any memories Jack had of the anger and loss of being separated from his children for two years were now extinguished in this unpredicted moment of Marbry's vulnerability.

Tenderly, Jack retorted, "No...I have failed...I should have paid more attention to what you wanted than what I wanted... I—I —"

She cut Jack off. "No, Jack, you did that, and more... You were just silly to think that I was more than I was. There was so much that needed to be healed, so much that you, that nobody, could undo with the duplicity of my family."

"That didn't matter to me, Marbry; I loved you, I didn't have to love your family."

"I knew that, but you were such a threat to them. It was so wrong they saw you as a threat...you knew that, but you could never see that in your pure, unadulterated, and damn naive mind."

"It's okay, Marbry..."

"They could never see how a person could be so honest, so comfortable in his own skin...that you existed as you were without a cloak of deceit, without a masquerade...Jack, that was way too much for the Wellingtons."

"Marbry, there were some wonderful things about your family..."

"Name them...okay, two, Cooper, Addison...but look what they tried to do with them...making my pure loving brother Cooper out to be some sort of freak, and sending my happy, energetic brother Addison away...I'm just so blessed that he got help with his substance abuse, and you know you were his role model, Jack. You don't have the slightest idea of how you helped him," Marbry said through floods of tears.

Jack felt now the tears streaming down on his end.

"Jack, I was walking through Little Portugal today...I thought of when I first took you there and we heard Leonard Cohen sing 'Suzanne.'"

"I remember it well."

"Remember we walked down the Blvd. St. Laurent and you kept singing the words from 'Suzanne.' You kept repeating 'Suzanne takes you down to her place near the river, you can hear the boats go by, you can spend the night beside her, and you know she's half crazy'...Jack...I thought you knew I was half crazy..."

With no effort to parallel the tender memory, Jack spat out, "No, I was half crazy, totally crazy about you..." They were both crying now.

"Oh, Jack, you tried, I tried, our children are beautiful...but I've done some terrible things."

"Marbry, I want to tell you the crazy things I've done."

Jack wanted to spill his guts about his bouts with drinking and his visit with Daisy, he wanted to tell all, but Marbry chimed in, "Jack, your terrible is not the terrible I'm sure that I am involved in... Jack, you are a beautiful man and you did 'touch me with your mind,' as Cohen sang."

"Marbry, we need to speak about the plans for our children…"

"Jack, you will be with them. Helene is real, like you, Jack, she always was, and my family and I did terrible things to her as well… You need to be with somebody like that… Jack, I have to go…"

"Marbry, should we talk through our lawyers…how should we go about this?"

In a fading voice, Marbry solemnly said, "Jack, there will be no lawyers for this. You'll make everything right, as you have always done. Thank you, thank you, goodbye."

"Marbry, wait, thank you for this, Marbry…" Jack could only hear the click of the phone.

Marguerite knocked on his door as she had almost three decades prior when Jack had made his fateful decision to change the course of his life.

"Everything all right, Jack?"

"Mom, I'm not sure, but I'll explain when I get back from Bellingham, as I'm leaving early."

"Okay, good night."

Jack could not sleep the whole night…he could not wrestle with Marbry's tone of despair. He would call Cooper after his meeting down in Bellingham.

Driving down I-5, Jack somehow anticipated bad news. Detective Flaherty delivered the expected.

Laying out a thick file on a wooden table in an auxiliary room at the Bellingham Police Department, Flaherty neatly positioned the contents in rows of surveillance pictures and papers stamped with "WELLCAOP" and "WELLUSOP." The letters stood for "Wellington Canada Operation" and "Wellington United States Operation." It wasn't until Jack picked up the surveillance photos, the type he would see on the cover of a *National Enquirer* newspaper, that he realized they were mostly of Marbry, her sister Christiana, a man identified as "Clive Sanders," and always a fourth male figure, most of them of Mid-Eastern descent. Jack stared at the picture of the man identified as "Clive." Sure enough, his hair now shorn and gray, it was the guy "around campus" whom Marbry, back in the day, had gotten her fake IDs from to get in the twenty-one-plus bars in Montreal.

"You're staring at the picture of Sanders, Mr. McKenna, can I ask why?"

"Well, I can't bear myself to look at these pictures of my ex-wife, as she obviously is involved in something treacherous…but," he said, pointing to Sanders, "I want to know the relationship of this dirtbag to her."

"Let me start by telling you your word 'treacherous' is correct. Your ex-wife, her sister, as you recognize here, and that man you recognize have been involved in an identity-theft ring. The man, Sanders, has been what we have determined at this point to be the mastermind. He has a dossier of petty crime going back to the seventies!"

"Come a long way from producing fake college IDs," Jack commented.

"So you are aware of how it started?"

Staring blankly at the detective, Jack angrily said, "I have no idea how any of this started or that it even existed."

"Apologies, Mr. McKenna, we did determine that a while ago…what I meant is…"

"I know what you meant; apologies accepted."

"Five years ago, the RCMP were onto Mrs. McKenna's— excuse me, as that time that's who she legally was…"

"Go on...I know that well..."

"Anyway, she and her sister and Sanders were exposed as stolen-ID traffickers. They had quite a network, going mostly in and out of the NY-Canadian border. They had a well-protected safe house in Massena, New York, complete with a resident hacker, who was graduated from R.P.I. in Troy, New York. Joint Canadian-U.S. law-enforcement officials combined on a tip to crack into the house and arrest the foursome. The hacker was the only one present, but that was a blessing in disguise as he, even before any immunity deal was set up, let us onto their passing on of stolen IDs to alleged terrorists. We knew we had them, and that we had him to testify against them, but a week later he hung himself. That worked out actually better for the investigation, as we were now able to key in and get evidence of the other three actually passing on the IDs to noted terrorists."

Jack was speechless.

"Mr. McKenna, we have two task forces from two different nations. We have information that they are meeting up with an American ISIS sympathizer and his handler, Abdullo Darvish, in Rochester, New York...we are going after them hard, as they are known to be heavily weaponized. Mr. McKenna, your ex-wife, will be caught and faces a lifetime in jail. But I want to tell you, lately she has expressed to her partners in crime that she wants out. We know that because we have a wiretap on her phones, her car, everywhere. I'm sorry; we do have your phone call from last night recorded."

"Can we make a deal to get a confession from her? You must know, then, she is contrite, and..."

Flaherty spewed back, "Both countries have what they want...it's too late...she's been in thick, she's been in long. The only thing I can offer, as a father, is to protect your children, remind them of what and who she once was."

"I'm not sure what that was, but yes, that's what I'll do."

Epilogue

WE WERE ALL STUNNED BY the news, the arrest, the sentencing of Marbry. We all loved her, but as a young child even I could sense the sadness, the emptiness. My step-brother, Benn, and my step-sister, Agnes-Marie, seemed to accept their parents' fate in the same way we, my brothers Scotty and Alex and I, accepted our own father's imprisonment, content to remember only the laughs. That's what Jack told us to hold on to, the moments of family sharing together.

With the Canadian and U.S. authorities arguing over jurisdiction, the trial took over two years to come together. Jack would visit Marbry on a regular basis in prison.

We were now all under one roof, Jack, my mother, Helene, my brothers, Benn, and Agnes-Marie, in Vancouver. The glue that got us together, or so it seems to me, was my mother's ability to get Jack to get counseling to stop his drinking that she thought we "didn't know about." It was pretty obvious, as he went from a fat man to a grey-haired guy who once again resembled an athlete. The Rockets franchise was resurrected, financed by Jack's old friend Bill Bensen, and Jack was named their new coach. My mother and he now made Bennett's organization, *Cyclists Serving Others*, worldwide, raising three point five million dollars for various charities.

Finally, with the trial over, Marbry was due for sentencing. I remember hearing that Jack, ever the optimist, and there at every day of the trial with Marbry, told her that "we will visit you constantly."

Marbry grew up in the shadow of betrayal. She ultimately embraced it, sullying the beauty of what I heard my stepdad describe as the "soul of her Montreal snow-white skin and scissor-sharp intellect." That soul was swallowed, I'm sure, by the final betrayal she had to endure. Christiana, in a plea agreement with the government that would garner her a lighter sentence, gave state's evidence against her very own sister. The federal authorities had been informed by her that "Marbry was the mastermind of the operation and set up the whole Rochester meet." We all knew, as did everyone in Quebec with a pulse, who had lured whom. Perhaps the judge also felt some empathy for Marbry's outcome. In a rare move that astonished court observers, the judge, "citing "exceptional circumstances related to her mother's health," issued her bail pending her sentencing. Marbry would go home to say her goodbyes to her family.

The accident was almost too much for even us to bear. It was two days before she was supposed to report for sentencing. It was a stone gray, depressing November day. Agnes-Marie, ever the tomboy, was skating on the back-pond ice adjoining our property. Listening to the radio, my mother called to me. "Rae-Ann," she said, "you will be the one to lead us in prayers." Marbry had driven off Highway 117, off one of the only cliffs on the highway.

What I remember most is how all of Jack's old teammates from Coquitlam, along with Arne and Bill, were there for us at the funeral. No matter where their lives had taken them, they always stayed close. When a cadre of young boys and girls proudly wearing the *Cyclists Serving Others* shirts came in, filling the pews, Priscilla, turning to Tom and Rachel, said, "Bennett's now here with all of us." Perhaps in a snow-covered pond, perhaps in a faraway rink on some lonely billet, perhaps in a Greyhound bus station in some isolated town, the loyalty of friendship forged through passion of purpose will always surmount suffering.

Made in the USA
Lexington, KY
18 March 2018